THE BOTHY BREW
AND
OTHER STORIES

HAMISH BROWN

First Edition 1993

The publisher acknowledges subsidy from the Scottish Arts Council towards the publication of this volume.

Typeset and Designed by Luath Press.
Printed and Bound by Dynevor Printing, Llandybie, Dyfed.

THE BOTHY BREW

AND

OTHER STORIES

BY

Hamish Brown

Luath Press Ltd.
Barr, Ayrshire KA26 9TN

OTHER PUBLICATIONS BY
HAMISH BROWN

Hamish's Mountain Walk 1978. *Gollancz* 1978 Paperback *Paladin* 1980

Hamish's Groats End Walk 1981. *Gollancz* 1981 Paperback *Paladin* 1983

Eye To The Hill (poems) *Pettycur Publishing* 1982

Time Gentlemen (poems) *Aberdeen University Press* 1983

The Great Walking Adventure. *Oxford University Press* 1983

Travels. *Scotsman/Geo. Sutherland* 1986

Hamish Brown's Scotland. *AUP* 1988

Climbing The Corbetts. *Gollancz* 1988

Rhum. *Cicerone Press* 1988

Great Walks, Scotland (with McOwan and Mearns) *Ward Lock* 1989

Scotland Coast To Coast. *Patrick Stevens* 1990

Walking the Summits Of Somerset And Avon. *Patrick Stephens* 1991

From the Pennines To The Highlands. *Lochar* 1992

Fort William And Glen Coe Walks. *Jarrold/O.S.* 1992

Edited: Poems Of The Scottish Hills. *AUP* 1982

Speak To The Hills (Poetry Anthology) *AUP* 1985

Bell's Scottish Climbs. *Gollancz* 1988

The Corbetts And Other Scottish Hills. *SMC* 1990

In Preparation: A Fife Coast Walk. (The Bridges to St. Andrews.)

INTRODUCTION

The short story has always been one of my favourite forms of reading for pleasure (I'd love to compile an anthology of the stories I've most enjoyed) so it is not surprising I've written many myself over the years. This is a selection, mainly of those with Scottish settings or interest, (but with the Alps or Morocco appearing too) most of which have been published in some form before, some in magazines, alas, no longer with us. Oldies will remember *The Bulletin* with affection, and *Blackwood's Magazine* published both fiction and travel pieces, causing at least one amusing confusion.

I'd written a story, set in the Alps, where the narrator, one Arthur, mentions a fiancée. A distant Canadian cousin, reading this, sent congratulations, best wishes and a present for my wedding! *Tait's tomb* I sent to *The Countryman*, saying it was a story but that they might like to use it. They did, and I had letters from all over the world telling of similar happenings, and, when I sent these to the Editor, he was not amused: he had taken it at face value too! At that time I was taking parties of youngsters into the wilds, and either told or read them stories at night round the bothy fires (so few had that experience at home) and *Tait's Tomb* grew out of the demand for "A spooky story, sir". Not surprisingly, several stories have youthful backgrounds. Nobody escapes the pains of growing up!

Sometimes I become annoyed at modern stories because there seems to be a constant, and false, over-concentration on the gratuitous vileness of the human condition. Not everybody lives in slums, most people never murder anyone, and they laugh and cry at minor, but no less real, aspects of life. That some of these stories were taken as true bears out my (and other's) delight in the sheer quirkiness of life. That is my subject, I suppose. ''Here's tae us! Wha's like us?''

These stories have appeared in a range of publications and my thanks go to editors past and present for permission to use them.

Alpine Journal, Blackwood's Magazine, The Bulletin, Climber and Hillwalker, The Countryman, Cycling World, Dollar Magazine, Glasgow Herald, The Great Outdoors, High, New Writing, Scotland, Rod and Line, The Scots Magazine, The Scotsman, Scottish Field, Weekend Telegraph, Words, and *Five Bird Stories* (Pettycur Publishing) and *Hamish Brown's Scotland* (Aberdeen University Press.)

I would also like to thank John Mitchell for his evocative drawings.

Hamish Brown, Kinghorn, 1993.

CONTENTS

THE BOTHY BREW

They had already become aware of the snow falling. The interior of the bothy had grown dim to the extent that they had had to stop reading their books. They lay, half inside their sleeping bags, chatting as climbers can from many shared intimacies.

"Your turn to make a brew" Gordon eventually commented. "It's getting right cold."

Reluctantly Ben swung his lanky legs over the bedshelf and wiggled his bare feet into the clammy depths of his plastic boots with their enveloping Yeti gaiters. He clattered over to the concrete table with its grime of soot and candle grease. The window that half-lit the table and the cell-like bothy was patterned with frost fronds. They, rather nostalgically, reminded Ben of the frieze of palm fronds he'd looked at when sleeping out in the Atlas Mountains a few weeks previously. He pressed a thumb against the glass and thawed out a spy hole. The snow raced past, from left to right, then from right to left, a maelstrom of malevolent power.

"Mm?" Gordon queried.

"Snowing hard. Nothing will be in condition the morn. Might as well eat everything the night and flog out in the morning."

"We've a lot of tins still. We can't eat all their weight the night. An the climbing gear weighs a ton. We could stay on."

"Humph" came Ben's unenthusiastic response.

"Maybe I should hae brought ma chanter only instead o the pipes. Saved weight."

"You're no practising in here," Ben yelped in alarm. "I've been deefened by your pipes ower often. You could dee of over-exposure to bagpipes."

"You've enjoyed them often enough," Gordon retorted. "Get the brew on anyway.

"There's no enough water."

"Tough!"

Gordon grinned from the assured comfort of his pit. Ben muttered to himself as he pulled on his duvet. The burn was only twenty yards off but that was far enough in the conditions. He made a strange sight with his top half bulging in red duvet padding above his long, thin legs clad only in old woolly long Johns he'd rescued from his late father's possessions. The Yeti gaiters flapped about his lower legs as he stomped to the door in his unlaced boots. He tugged open the door. An icy draught swirled in a feathering of white from the horizontal flow. Gordon grinned again. Ben noticed and his inward scowl turned to outward banter.

"I may be gone for some time, Captain Scott."

He slipped out, but the door remained open and the snow kept swirling in. Gordon called his partner a fairly rude name and reluctantly tiptoed over in stocking soles to slam the door. He stood on a wet patch and swore again. He stood irresolute on one foot. It was too early for supper. There was not enough wood to justify an early fire. The gloom of dusk was rapidly darkening the gloom of the storm. He picked a dry route back to the bedshelf and lay on top of his bag. At least he wasn't out there fetching the water. He opened the case with his pipes. Maybe he'd give Ben a welcome back. What about the reel *You're A Long Time Awa?* or *Weary With Waiting?*

They'd been lucky to get their new route in that day. The ribbon of ice which periodically formed down the middle of the great slabs of The Ashet was a desirable "plum".

"Like The Curtain, only bigger," Ben had described it. They'd been happily back in the bothy before the gathering blackness had eventually broken into heavy snowfall. Ben had vetoed Gordon playing a celebratory tune on the pipes inside the bothy. He'd rather pointedly suggested calling the new route "Drone".

The storm bullied Ben to the burn. He had quite a job to stop on its banks and his hands began to freeze at once as he pushed the awkward top of the squashy water carrier under the surface. The stones sticking up above water level had already donned a polar-bear furring of white. Even with his back to the snow his specs became slobbery wet and the blast was icily attaching flake after flake to his woolly bottom.

By the time the gallon container was half-full he'd had enough. He rose, turned, and a blast caught him just as his foot was skiting on the bank. He sprawled, landing hard on one knee and dropping the water carrier. He grabbed it before it had given more than a couple of gurgles. He jammed his glasses in a pocket and staggered off for the cosy bothy in a fairly disgruntled mood.

"What some people will do for a cup of tea," he thought. "Gordon can dae what he likes. I'm having a dram first. Bloody bothy."

A few seconds later he repeated the last comment aloud, then yelled "Where is the bloody bothy?"

He stopped. In the grey gloom of dusk he could see nothing beyond the speckled swirl of snowflakes, greyer dots that danced out of nowhere in their thousands like bees swarming from an upset hive. They fluttered into his face, an irritating, cobwebby touch, they flew into his gasping mouth, they tickled into his eyes so he stood blinking myopically.

"Must hae passed it," he muttered.

He turned back, just able to make out his tracks which were filling with drift. He took a dozen steps then stopped again, peering and blinking about him. He shaded his eyes with a cold hand. There was no sign of the bothy.

Ben didn't panic. He'd survived epics enough to accept problems as climbers had to. Every situation of panic, accident or disaster had its best solution, its natural procedure under the circumstance. It was something that he and Gordon, regular climbing partners over twenty years, had talked about often enough. It led them to scorn, rightly, the simplistic teachings of 'rules'. The hills could aye come up with situations not covered by the book. He smiled grimly. The book certainly didn't cover the situation of standing lost in your long Johns in a blizzard a few yards from safety.

Ben realised the seriousness of his situation at once. (There were several missing tips to his toes from an experience on an unplanned bivouac on Nanda Devi.) He could not even be sure, if he had walked past the bothy, whether he would have done so past its front or along the back. In other words, the bothy could be in any direction.

He laid down the water carrier and blew into his chilled fingers, his mind racing to cope with the crisis. He could hardly see now (without specs, his eyesight was not very good at the best of times) for the gloom reduced everything to a blur of gyrating grey. He set off, trying to follow his track back to the burn in the hope of discovering his original bothy-to-burn prints. After half a dozen steps he knew he wasn't on any track. Contact had completely gone.

Ben was by then shivering violently. He abandoned the water carrier and crammed his numb hands into his duvet pockets then took them out again to lace his boots and zip up the gaiters. His fingers were so stiff he could hardly tie the cord round their tops. Shelter was the desperate priority, but shelter was unlikely. Others had perished in like circumstances, he knew. You could burrow into old snow, maybe, but with new powder you could do nothing. There was not even a gully or boulder near the bothy that could give him shelter. Movement alone would help him, temporarily at least, till the insidious fingers of hypothermia would tease life itself from his failing grasp. Ben ran.

He ran blindly (in more senses than one), he ran, and jumped and spun, in a frenzy of activity and gradually a certain warmth eased back into his frozen limbs. His ears burned, his fingers ached with a return to feeling, his bladder throbbed so he had to relieve its tension. He rejoiced at the restored feeling -- but his gambler's gallop had not led him to chancing on the bothy. The cold immediately gripped his half-clad frame again. He set off on another wild run.

All too soon he had to pause, gasping for breath, the wretched snowflakes being sucked into his lungs, his face red with exertion yet at the same time his nose and ears tingling with frostnip rather than blood-warmth. Three more times he careered about in search of the bothy, in search of body-warmth. Each time he stopped sooner, froze quicker, while the spectre of reality shrieked in his brain as the wind screamed in the world about him. He was going to die. It was ridiculous. It was infuriating. It was overwhelmingly sad.

He did not want to die.

Yet he was realist enough to recognise his mortal danger. When he ultimately became too exhausted to keep warm by physical exertion he was doomed. When the heart could no longer flush the surface of his body with warmth the cold would win. He would drift off into a last, gentle sleep. It would not be painful, like lying broken below the Orion Face (as friend Tony had died) but the cold would burrow inwards to the core of his body and the heart-pump would fail. He'd lectured about exposure often enough. He knew. He knew.

Should he just give up, he wondered? Why prolong the process? He could hardly think straight any longer, but the lust for life drove him again and again into renewed but diminishing bursts of activity. He was a human robot, programmed for life, but with the parts worn out and failing. He felt tears wet his cheeks but when he put up a hand to wipe them away he could feel nothing. His hand might as well have been made of wood. The wet turned to stars of ice on his wet cheeks.

He decided some form of hallucination was part of this sleepy disintegration for he could hear spectral music through the storm. A jig of death. He thought of Saint-Saëns. But then, like a dream recalled, he realised the tune was a march, one he recognised as *The Macmillans of Arkaig*, which Gordon had composed for the Oban Mod. Gordon? Good God! It was Gordon playing his pipes. In a last surge of energy he staggered towards the sound.

In a few steps he came up against a wall. He could not grasp its significance for a moment. It was simply a cruel barrier. He hammered at it with his wooden fists so cornflakes of snow sprayed off the grey granite. "Let me by! Let me by!," he sobbed. Then it dawned. It was the wall of the bothy. He groped his way along it in the direction of the wind-lilting sound.

Gordon stood in the doorway, red-faced, a figure of ridiculous unreality in his underwear, a foot tapping out the rhythm ("trying tae stop ma bloody toes freezin.") As Ben fell towards him there was a dying wail from the pipes. Gordon caught him and, as he was dragging Ben across to the bedshelf the casualty opened his eyes and tried to speak. Gordon bent to listen.

"Mind, I once said you could play yir pipes at ma funeral?"

Gordon nodded.

"Well, you near did, pal...."

That was thanks of a sort, Gordon supposed. In the end it was he who had to make the bothy brew.

SÉRACS

Over-investment in machinery brought about the financial crisis in Danny Peplinska's scrap yard on Firth Street East. Danny loved handling the cool, metallic atoms and could never resist a machine that could cut, flatten or melt the metals he recycled from our waste society. When an out-of-breath jogger stopped at his gate Danny noticed his interest and invited him in to see round the yard.

Ivor Bentley-Crowcombe, a popular artist in his own right, ran an internationally-renowned gallery of modern art in Bristol, but was frequently gallivanting about Britain, Europe and America. Ivor had studied at Grenoble in his early twenties and had climbed in the Dauphiné regularly, but the only reminders of those days were the many mountain paintings and sculptures he had acquired.

One day his wife had commented that he was "becoming as broad in the beam as he was in the brain" so, piqued, every day since he had dutifully put in a run, no matter where he was, no matter how tight his schedule.

Ivor had been visiting the friendly Kirkcaldy Art Gallery, officially to discuss a coming exhibition, unofficially to drool over the extensive collection of Peploes, so it was late afternoon before he set off along the sands under the Esplanade. The tide forced him off the shore and he then found himself toiling up an unexpectedly steep brae. He turned off -- and so came on Danny's yard.

He stood, breathless, fascinated by the weird tangle of shapes, the unintentional geometrics, the frightful grace of powerful machinery. "Must be money in scrap" ran through his mind, art and finance being the right and left ventricles of his existence. He gladly followed Danny round the yard.

One machine was effortlessly slicing thick power cable. ("The Knowles Cutter goes through it like butter" Danny chirped), a man in goggles was cutting inch-thick iron plate with a blue flame, a furnace suddenly opened and lava flowed. Ivor walked in awe. He could quite understand Danny's fascination with the job. Suddenly he stopped.

Before him was a stack of cubes of what looked like tangled and crushed silver snakes. They were beautiful. They were desirable. Danny smirked: "Aluminium core: stripped by the Vortex, cut by the Baby Knowles, cubed by the Sondheimer Press." In Ivor's eyes, however, they appeared as objects born of the high Alps: bold chunks of glacial ice, sculpted by time and motion. Beautiful indeed.

"How much?" Ivor blurted out and was soon deep in an aspect of the business which he never underestimated. The next day his overloaded Transit headed south while Danny was left chuckling over a £300 windfall (which he badly needed). Ivor made three groupings out of his haul, welding the aluminium in places (not easy) and finally callling them 'Séracs I, II and III.'

'Séracs I' he set up on his own patio in the Cotswolds and 'Séracs II' went to the gallery in Bristol of course.

'Séracs III' was dispatched to London, with a stylish coloured brochure showing Alpine glaciers, an appropriate modern poem and pictures of the various stages of his work on the sculpture. 'Séracs III' was snatched up at once by an American collector for a bargain £30,000.

On the same day as 'Séracs III' was sold Danny Peplinska was officially declared bankrupt.

THE BLONDE

I will definitely, for sure, kill any bastard who lays a finger on her. The Blonde. The beautiful blonde who comes past my kiosk every day and gives me that smile. Her passing is the highlight of my life. That's what I said to myself. Many times. Got quite possessive really.

Don't know where she came from. I don't hear much village gossip living down in my cell by the harbour but I sees everything and hears everything. The things people get up to in cars -- as if they were invisible. I could tell you stories. Disgusting. And then there's the bikers. They scare the shit out of me. They think they own the place when they come. *The Anchor* boss hates them too but he can't pick his customers no more than me. Ten-to-one they park just outside the car park and clutter the place up for everyone. To save ten pence a bike -- and then you see them stagger out of *The Anchor* with bottles and bottles that cost the earth. Everyone hates them because they're afraid. Sure I'm shit scared but they never bother me. I'm just 'The Weed' to them. Just the car park attendant. But just let them try any hanky panky and they'll find out. I keep a gun behind the cash tray in the drawer. Have for years -- but that's another story.

Sometimes I dreams of this. Their coarse faces at the grille. "Hand the money over, Weed, -- or we'll beat you to pulp!" and I'll smile and reach in and they'll smile in expectancy -- till I bring out the gun. "It will happen one day, sure as death," I used to tell myself. "Then the Weed will turn." That's not right, but you know what I mean. We can all be pushed too far.

Not that I owe much loyalty to the Council. Not on the pittance they pay me for the long hours. And I've put up with it for ten years. 'Put up with it' is not right, either. I quite like the job. What else would suit a queer sod like me? And don't get that wrong either. I'm not queer in *that* sense. I see their filthy goings-on, too in the car park. And there's one lot every summer comes and swims off the end of the bay, bare naked, only swimming's not all they do. Think

they can't be seen but I've good ex-navy binocs. And see everything in my bay.

The road ends here. Just *The Anchor* and the car park. And Luigi's ice cream van in summer. Luigi's all right. I let him park for free where everyone has to walk past his van. I give him coffee too, and he lets me have ice cream or cold drinks. Not that I often want cold drinks. Not in my rotten state of health.

No, I'm not queer. Just an accident, with a face like a fucking monkey and a misshapen body. Oh, I used to save for a month and go and have it off with the prossie up the road, but who wants sex with a hunchback? So I hang on here. It's something. I see it all from the windows of my cabin or the windows of my flat above the back of the car park. 'Flat' was the Council's grand word for it: a two-room-and-a-loo concrete prison left over from the wartime defences. But it's mine. And I can watch the beach twenty four hours a day. It's my beach.

There's all sorts of regulars. Retired men who poke with their walking sticks, a fat woman who paddles every day, her skirt tucked into pink bloomers, the fitness freaks and joggers -- and the dog owners. I hate the dogs too. They take them there to crap and pretend not to see it happening. Then the kids come and play next day. Disgusting.

I like watching the kids. It's one of the few places they can still be kids and have fun for nothing. A bucket and spade maybe. A model car. A fishing net on a bamboo cane. You don't need much else. And Luigi makes sure they don't drop litter. "Not on my beach!" he yells. I don't mind. He can call it his beach. But it's really mine. I'm always here. He lives -- somewhere, I suppose. Not here.

I like watching the dollybirds. Especially her. The blonde. She is beautiful and always gives me a smile or a wave when she passes. Every morning. I reckon she works in the next village for you could set your watch by her appearance each morning. 08.25. The sudden clack-clacking of her high heels as she passes *The Anchor*, then my thrill of suddenly seeing what she'll be wearing. Very fashion-conscious. But not swanky. Self-possessed. Poised. She stops at the steps, kicks off her shoes, gives me a wave, and goes down onto the sand to walk barefoot along and round the rocks out of sight.

I've known her for a year now. Every little detail. Her hair styles. Touch of make-up. Clothes. Jewellry. All perfect. Big but graceful she was. I could imagine she'd be super-efficient at her job, whatever it was. Office obviously. She'd drive me to distraction if I was her boss. She drove me to distraction and I was nothing at all. Her smile to the grille. Her wave. When she waved and smiled that was sunshine on the bleakest of my bad days. I had a lot of black days. She was the most important thing in my life.

At weekends or on summer evenings she'd sometimes come down to lie on the beach, or swim. I'd keep on eye on her. Not spying, but protective like. Mind, at nights, I could let my imagination go. I bet she was cool through and through. One day as she bent down to take off her shoes her boobs popped right out of her dress. Did she panic? Not a bit of it. She finished taking off her shoes, then stood up, adjusted things, gave me my wave and smile, same as ever, and went down onto the sand. Cool. Clothed or naked would make no difference between us. If I asked her she'd probably strip off like a model she was that cool. But no way would I ask of course.

I'd watched her come down to the bay late one afternoon. Sandals. Apricot-coloured two-piece suit thing. Fair hair let loose and flowing out in waves at each step. Picnic basket. Each detail was photographed on my memory. I could give the police a perfect description of her, any time.

Then four louts came on bikes. Mischief-makers, their sex tickled by the ride, their courage to be topped-up with booze in *The Anchor.* What might they not get up to? They'd better not go near The Blonde. Seeing me scowling from the door of my hut one of them gave me the fingers before they piled noisily into the pub. Maybe they're on drugs. You never know these days. Terrible.

I pulled open the drawer and counted up my day's takings. Wouldn't be any more. But I waited. After all *she* was out there, in the gloaming, alone, and those four were in there. You read about things in the paper (I didn't have TV.) The very thought of rape made me sweat. Women were sacred. The Blonde especially. Suddenly it struck me that I never even knew her name. I'd waved to her 378 times and never even knew her name.

The stars were already sneaking into the sky. And one seemed to be flickering at the end of the sand. A bonfire. My Blonde had lit a bonfire. Above it a red planet glowed -- the signal on the railway track. I like early night. Often stood to watch before going into my cell block of a flat.

Shit! The peace was broken by the bloody bikers. They were obviously tanked. Shouting. Every other word fucking something or other. They didn't give a damn for anything or anybody. I'd quietly shut the door in case my booth became a target. It had been broken into more than once -- but I always cleared the drawer before going home. I took out the gun and sat in sweaty fear, watching the louts through the grille. One unzipped and began peeing into the basin of the drinking fountain. One of his mates gave him a shove. Animals!

Then one said, "Let's go along the sand".

"Hey, it would be a good place to bring the birds."

"Nice and quiet."

As they tumbled down the steps another shouted about just what he'd like to do to a girl if he could lay hands on one right then. My hair stood up on end at this for *she* was out there on the sand. She could be poised, self-assured, but not with four drunken louts dying to pull the trigger. They'd fuck her for sure.

Well, let them try. I'd do some pulling the trigger -- and not in the way they would be meaning. For real. Let one of them lay a finger on her and I'd kill the sod.

I could hear their raucous voices from along the sands and then I thought I heard a scream. That did it. I raced along by my flat to get along the dunes and come on them quickly and unseen. I crept down by the rocks and then stepped out with the gun pointing at the laughing, milling group.

One of them was naked and stood holding his willy. Guilty as hell. He looked up and for one second saw what was coming.

Disbelief and terror flitted across his face before the bullet tore into his body throwing him over backwards. (I told you I'd do it!) His mates scarpered off and I fired two more shots after them into the dark. But I was concerned about *her.* I couldn't see her. What the hell had they done? Where was she?

God knows where my shot had hit the rapist. His whole front was a bloody mess. He lay moaning in a rhythm that sounded indecent. Furious, I picked a heavy piece of wood from the fire and rammed the glowing end into his crotch. "You bastard! You fucking rapist! Where is she? Where is she?"

"What are you raving about," he screamed.

"The girl. The Blonde. Where is she?

"What girl?"

"The only girl. The one you were...." I couldn't even say it. Instead I rammed the wood into his groin again. He scrabbled at the wood, screaming wordlessly and, to shut him up, I lifted it and brought it down on his face. Again. And again. Until there was no face and no voice. Even if I hadn't killed the swine he'd never, ever, have done anyone again. Real justice.

I wanted to cry out a name. But I didn't know her name. I was frantic. I spent ten minutes hurrying about among the rocks looking for their victim but found no one. No female clothes. Had they buried her in the sand? Not murder surely? Not *her!* Or had she escaped in the turmoil? I'd just have to wait and see. When it was light. It was too confusing in the dark.

I collected all the clothes and leathers from the sand and took them up among the elderberry bushes growing behind the dunes to bury them deeply. I also wiped the gun and buried it separately. I then took off all my clothes (something I'd never do in public) and dragged the body down into the sea. The white foam turned pink I noticed. I waded a long way out, till the water was up to my neck, brought the one I'd sentenced round and pushed him off to sea. By morning he'd be miles away and might never even come ashore again. Not that I cared, either way.

For half an hour I sat to dry-off, brooding by the dying embers. The tide came in steadily, wiping away all the scuffs on the sand. In the end it bore off a few charred pieces of driftwood. I went back to my cell and collapsed into a deep sleep, drained by my executioner's role. I'd not done anything like that before.

My sleep was so deep that I nearly overslept. I had to open up for 08.30 and didn't even have time to make tea. So, I decided I'd open up and then go along the sands and see if I could find the girl. The Blonde. I could hardly bear to think of her. She might be lying along there, shamed and naked. Nobody must ever see that!

It wasn't yet half past when I looked at my watch. 08.25. God! *Her* time. I heard the clack-clacking of her high heels as the sound echoed off the pub front in my imagination. I looked for my vision to appear. There she was. In buttercup-bright blouse and blue slacks, a blue comb thing in her hair, duffle over her shoulder. I could have sworn she was real!

At the top of the steps she paused to take off her fancy shoes. I tried to get my heated imagination to replay that happy time when her breasts fell free. I tried to make it happen. But nothing happened. And, as she smiled and waved to me and set off down to the sand, I suddenly realised she was off to work as usual, quite real, quite unharmed, as ravishingly beautiful as ever. The Blonde.

For the first time, in 379 occasions, I failed to wave back. I was a bit upset.

TOUR D'ECOSSE

Mrs. Dundas came bustling out of the Priorwood Garden gate and almost knocked the young lad over. Mrs. Dundas was always bustling, being, as she cheerfully admitted, 'bulky and busy' by nature, and, having spent a couple of hours working in the dried flowers shed (actually sitting down for two whole hours), she sailed out with the momentum of a man o' war heading to sea, quite failing to notice the wee boatie of a boy beneath her bows.

He was bowled over, giving his head a good dunt on the road. He sat up, looked at Mrs. Dundas's startled face and immediately went horizontal again, letting out a long moan, 'quite bovine' she was to describe it later in all the glory of having a real story to tell to her friends, and, better still, un-friends.

A small crowd soon gathered, all offering conflicting advice which showed few had ever attended first aid classes, but the real panic soon went out of the situation as the young man sat up. He looked a bit strange (he looked quite normal really; he just happened to be a foreigner) and his first words were a rapid repetition of "Bicycle. Bicycle. Bicycle."

"No, dear" Mrs. Dundas boomed. "You weren't hit by a bicycle. I'm afraid I bumped into you."

"Bicycle. My bicycle."

"Do you have a bicycle?"

"Yes. No!"

"What on earth do you mean?"

"Police!"

"Don't you think he's a bit concussed, Mrs. Dundas?" someone said. "Shouldn't we get the doctor?"

"No doctor plees," the youngster pleaded as he tried to rise. "I want police. Police!"

"Police" echoed Mrs. Dundas with a slightly apprehensive catch in her throat. "Why do you want the police?"

"My bike is stolen."

"But you didn't have a bike when I ran over -- ran into you."

"No, it was stolen before accident. I leave in car park, there (he pointed across Buccleuch Street). Then I go see historic ab..ab.. historic building there" (he waved down Abbey Street) then gave another groan and sank his head in his hands. "*J'ai mal à la tête.*" He seemed almost in tears. Obviously a foreign tourist. Excitable no doubt.

"Do get the doctor," Mrs. Dundas asked of no-one in particular.

"He's on his way. The shop phoned."

The youth made it to his feet this time. He was quite a presentable young man really, if a bit thin, very blond and tanned, with black, clinging shorts and a shirt of rainbow colours. A sunshade hung on its elastic round his neck. Several people realised that he did have the appearance of a cyclist. The Border Three Hundred had gone through two weeks earlier and they had sported a kaleidoscope of colours. He looked just like them.

"What are you saying about a bike?" a man asked.

"Bike? Ah, **Yes**. Bike. Bicycle. My bicycle is stolen. Disappeared. I leave it chained O.K. I must meet police. *Comprenez?* Everything is gone: my clothes, money, passport." He groaned again. "Sorry, my head no good. Plees help. Police."

"You mean to say you've lost all your belongings?" Mrs. Dundas queried, obviously appalled.

The young lad nodded, then winced and held his hand to his head. "*Ma tête. Ma tête!*"

"It's disgraceful," Mrs. Dundas swelled. "And I have to knock you over at such a moment. Come! Come!" and she half dragged him up to the Market Square and along the High Street to the Police Station.

The doctor eventually caught up with proceedings there, by which time they were in the back room with Mrs. Dundas producing mugs of a dark, teabag brew for the youth, the sergeant and herself while the constable was busy giving the local patrol cars a description of the missing cycle, a *Mountain Regnant* no less, with red Karrimor panniers and a bar bag with an Olympus OM camera, money, passport and maps in it. The youth had visibly shrunk from the glaring officer.

"Sorry. Very stupid. I chain bike, very careful, but I forget to take the bag. Soon I want picture of ruins and remember so hurry back, very quick, but everything, everything gone."

His voice cracked, as well it might. It was quite a predicament for a youngster to find himself in. The sergeant merely sighed. It happened all the time. People were so bloody stupid.

Mrs. Dundas was thoroughly outraged. "But Willie, it happened here. I mean, it's the sort of thing one would expect in Gala, but not...."

The doctor's entry had interrupted the rest.

"Seems I'm not really needed. Could do with a cuppa though, Charlotte."

He examined the youth's skull. There was a good pullet's egg of a bump but that was all, he decided.

"You'll live, me lad."

"Did you hear what's happened to him?"

"Yes, Charlotte. It's a bit of a problem. Are you touring?" he asked the lad.

"Oui ! Yes. *Le tour d'Ecosse.* Borders, Glasgow, Burrell Collection, Lock Lomond. Edemboorg. I fly yesterday to Edemboorg. One night in *auberge* -- youth hostel -- then come here for maybe three nights in hostel. *Merde!* My card of membership she is stolen also."

"Oh, I'm sure Dougie will let you in or you can get a temporary one."

"But my money is disappeared, except for small money," and he pulled out a couple of crumpled notes and a pickle of coins.

"We'll just have to organise for him," Mrs. Dundas said, in a tone which was all too familiar to the others. The sergeant muttered "Must see if Stenhouse had got round the cars", and sidled into the front office with the doctor following after.

"Have to get on, Charlotte. Let me know what you come up with. Be glad to help., Good luck, young man. Cheerio."

The youth, Felix Vigan, really was completely destitute. He was a fourth year economics student at Lyon, he'd explained. His father was a professor in the language school there, and was off touring Turkey with Mme. Vigan. There was no other family. It would take some time to sort things out. Luckily there was a consulate in Edinburgh but it wouldn't be open over the weekend. The sergeant's half-joking, "We could aye give him a cell" did not go down well with Mrs. Dundas.

"Really, Willie, you lack all finer feelings," and it gave Charlotte a smug satisfaction to take a fiver off the sergeant as the first contribution to a whip-around as her initial step in community involvement.

Between the police station and the youth hostel she persuaded four people she knew, and two people she didn't, to part with some cash. Youth and £25 were deposited with Dougie at the youth hostel, and Mrs. Dundas sailed off, leaving a wake of purposeful content behind her. The honour of the town was adrift. And she was at the helm.

To be fair, Mrs. Dundas worked wonders. She personally went round half the town with a box for contributions, she involved many other people likewise. She collared the bank manager (at Marmion's Brasserie, being a Saturday night!), saw the local reporter who, in turn, called in a photographer after he'd met the unfortunate visitor.

"Sad-eyed, gentle Felix Vigan, a thousand miles from home; robbed, injured, and destitute", his piece started, and a well-posed photograph beautifully captured the pathos, so the story was grabbed

-19-

not only locally but by the papers in Edinburgh and even Glasgow! "A good sob story is an excellent runner-up to disasters or murder," the reporter grinned to his local radio compatriot in the bar of the King's Arms.

In some ways, like this, the action spread far out from Mrs. Dundas's initial kindly bow-wave of activity. Border people are indeed kind and generous and helped automatically. Dougie, the warden, gave him a new membership card and quietly paid for it himself. His wife pressed food on the lad. People brought clothes. And money poured in. Mrs. Dundas said they, quite consciously and morally, would have to raise enough for an air ticket home *after* he'd had his planned holiday.

The Gala Town Cycle Shop generously gave Felix a mountain bike on loan for as long as he wanted. (The Junior Chamber bought new panniers.) The bike could be left at a brother's cycle shop in Edinburgh at the end, the proprietor suggested.

There was a lot of phoning to the consulate about arranging a new passport which could likewise be collected at the end of his tour. And A.T. Mays would have his ticket ready at their Turnhouse desk. All that was finalised on a day visit to Edinburgh in Mrs. Dundas's car. Felix found the journey quite terrifying. His mentor drove her Volvo as if it was a battleship.

When, a week later, Felix rode out of town it was quite an occasion. "Just like the Tour de France," he joked in his quiet way. "I am most honoured by all these gracious people", and he waved towards the crowd round the Market Square. Mrs. Dundas half smothered him with one of her generous hugs and stood, bright-eyed and happily righteous as he headed off along the cheering High Street for Abbotsford and the start of his tour.

The sergeant watched him pass. "The bugger's got enough money to stay at Five Star Hotels and use a chauffeur-driven Rolls". Constable Stenhouse smiled -- inwardly -- recalling who had contributed the first £5 of the Felix Vigan Fund.

Mrs. Dundas received a postcard from Loch Lomond, thanking

everyone again for their 'prodiferous generosity to a poor refugee'.

"Isn't he sweet?" she asked, showing the card to the doctor.

"No more than you've been, Charlotte," he replied diplomatically.

Everything appeared to have gone well. The bike was duly dropped off, passport and ticket collected and Felix Vigan flew home, which, for the good people of the Borders, was the end of the story.

"I had hoped for a card at Christmas," Mrs. Dundas was to remark later, "But maybe they don't go in for that sort of thing. Lovely boy. Lovely boy."

Lovely boy was spending quite a bit of his Christmas vacation dreaming about the following summer's trip. It would his last as a student. He'd enjoyed his successive free cycle tours in Ireland, Norway and Scotland. The Scots were bloody mean, of course. In Ireland and Norway he'd been given a new bike, not just one on loan. It had been tempting to flog it, but, what the hell, he'd come back with the equivalent of over 3,000 francs and he didn't want any queries following him home. He smirked, too, thinking of how he'd had that bonus of being knocked over by the big fat lady. He thought he'd played that rather well. Her conscience must have largely made Scotland the richest swindle of all. Silly thing, a conscience. He'd never had a conscience, no more than he'd ever had a bike. Ah well, it was all good practice for working in the Bourse. After all it was just the same, wasn't it, -- making money out of nothing?

THE BOY WHO SPOKE TO BIRDS

Mrs. Paton sat looking out over the grey sea, sat with her feet curled up on the sofa in a pose which was tense yet, at the same time, slovenly. She was tired but then she had been tired for years. Now, though, she was deeply anxious as well.

William would be five next birthday and then the shut-up fears and worries over him would have to come out. They should have long before now, but Mrs. Paton had always hoped things would change, had fervently looked for a miracle with the faith of despair. She felt like someone pushing against a door trying to bar entry to an intruder; it was push and counter-push, hope and despair, but with the defender weakening at every heave, till eventually the door would be forced open, her feet would scrabble and slide back to leave her lying on the floor like a crumpled rug. It was a nightmare image that came to her at night, destroying sleep, destroying rest. She was so very tired, so very tired.

Her head nodded, but immediately jerked up. She must not relax. Not with William. Where was he, anyway? She uncoiled quickly and peered down from the window over the barren little garden. William was there all right. She half smiled with relief, then froze.

William was holding out his hand and a bright-billed blackbird was pecking at the crust he held. The child was talking happily to the bold bird. Mrs. Paton sank back on the sofa and covered her face with her hands.

She did not break into tears. There was simply a long silence which ended with a sigh. She lay back again, staring into the grey sky, staring as if through its wintry curtaining she might glimpse a

fractured hint of spring. There had been springs -- when the world was all dancing green and love lit a thousand joys as sunrise lights the little waves. Her own childhood had been cheered with a mob of brothers and sisters, cousins and friends. She had assumed that life as she had known it in the warm south would continue for ever. Even when her stormy petrel, Randolph Paton, swooped down and bore her away to this harsher northern landscape she had laughed and accepted the adventure.

Was that only six years ago? Could six years so destroy a heart? a love? a life? It happened slowly enough, it felt at the time -- just like the dainty catspaws of the turning tide, each so gentle and solitary among the red ribs of sand, yet after a few hours the ebb had flowed and a million million gallons of North Sea waters had poured over the beach. That was the way she had slowly been engulfed.

Randolph had set up a comfy home, she was going to have a baby: it all seemed so marvellous. Then Randolph went off, leaving her ''secure'' in his erratic generosity, but mentally and spiritually battered. She was quite ill when William was born and out of her weakness had come this ghost child who seemed to only half belong to this world.

The burden had grown from the day of his difficult birth, this secret, strangling burden which she could not, would not, share. But William could not be hidden away indefinitely. Some people were aware already that he was a peculiar child: ''fey'' was how the old woman next door put it. Luckily this neighbour did not poke and pry, and there were no bungalows on the other side. Randolph had chosen this end house for its peace and its fine perch above the crumbling basalt cliff where the fulmars nested. It caught all the gales that blew up and down that coast, but Randolph had rather enjoyed that -- it was such a reflection of his own character. It was perhaps in character, too, that he had so shipwrecked her on his prow of land. It was all so very different from ''home'' as she had always known it. Here she felt the landscape, and seascape, were punishing her in some way. Had she been sensible she would have moved back to the friendly south, but somehow she did not have the drive to break out -- not after William was born anyway.

A shriek from the garden had her leaping to the window once more. It had been a yell of glee, however. William was circling the lawn with his wings, his arms rather, outstretched, and his golden head thrown back, laughing at the wheelings of a gull. Mrs. Paton sat down again, cringing into the sofa, her body the weary sign of her inner misery. Her eyes followed the gull as it wheeled and swung, rose, or hung on the sky. It mesmerised her. It bemused her. Now and then as a clear laugh came from her son, she flinched, the merest twitch outwardly, but inside, they were unconscious blows that were steadily driving her to the edge.

She roused herself suddenly, like a bird put to flight by the casual passing of a dog, and went to put on the kettle. She flitted about the kitchen restlessly, waiting for it to boil.

She recalled so clearly all the contributory episodes that had led up, hint on hint, to the present certainty. Long before he could walk, or even crawl very effectively, William had been fascinated by birds. He would sit for hours on the grass in the garden gurgling away at them or wander off into the shrubs after them. She had soon found that the best-loved dolls were not teddy bears but large, soft birds. She had made him several in felt colours -- rainbow-bright creatures with which she had hoped to buy back some of her rightful love. She had come to feel she was actually competing for affection -- with the very sparrows! She was both outraged and frightened.

Once, in a temper, she had hit William. He did not burst into wild tears like any normal three year old, but had fled to the window and sat pressed against the storm-lashed glass. His tears ran down like raindrops and he carried on a quiet, broken commentary to the thrush on the lawn. For days he hardly looked at her. Mrs. Paton had been very frightened.

She ran through to check again. William was still talking to the birds. Several cheeky blue tits were darting about in the honeysuckle above his head. With his bright curls and a skin almost as pale as those scented blossoms, surrounded by those dainty creatures, she thought he looked more unreal than ever -- a changeling or, rather, a cherub which had strayed from some Tiepolo chapel ceiling. He always looked so delicate, gentle as down which any breeze might blow away over the sea. She felt as if he was only on loan, that one day he would have vanished: reclaimed, flown off in the secret clarion of a dawn chorus.

The whistle of the kettle called her back to the kitchen. She made the tea and stood it to infuse. Where had she gone wrong with William? Even as she framed the recurring question she knew it was an unfair one. She had done no wrong. She had loved and cherished her son as any mother does. The fault -- oh! what a word! -- was William's. If only he could have been a normal child. She might have bounded back into life herself and made friends locally. William could have made friends. Instead she had to withdraw, to shut William up -- like a bird in a cage -- keeping themselves to themselves from the rest of the village. She was usually known, if at all, as "that strange woman with the pretty wee boy".

But soon William would have to go to school. He would be thrown into the battering light. She gave a little gasping cry at the thought, imagining him fluttering, broken-winged, for the shadowy bushes -- then cried "Damn", for once more she was picturing him as a bird. He was not a bird. He was her boy. **Her boy.** But she could hear the tormenting voices of other kids, their scornful reporting to their many mummies "Oh, yes, there's another new boy. William. He's daft. All he does is talk to birds".

William was not bad to his mother; he had a gentleness that knew nothing of ill-will and little of stormy emotions. He was biddable. But always with a remoteness that was harder to bear than any tantrum would have been. He literally belonged to the birds as much as to Mrs. Paton. He had once said, "Mummy, the birds speak to me", but she had been so upset that he had thereafter kept his worlds apart.

He could lie and watch TV on a a winter's night like any other child, but always there was a part of him seemingly detached, tuned to some avian wavelength. Once, in the middle of *Doctor Who*, he had turned to her and cried "It's lost, mummy! It's lost, mummy. And very cold and hungry". She had wondered what on earth he was talking about but had patiently put down her knitting and opened the backdoor at his urging. Lying on the snow, in the wedge of light, was an exhausted fieldfare.

Mrs. Paton carried her tea through on a tray. She had added a glass of juice for William. She looked out of the window but couldn't see the child. "Nesting among the rhoddies again" she sighed, this time consciously using the comparison, for even as she went out of the back door to call him, she was determining that something would have to be done. She would go to the doctor tomorrow. He was young and looked understanding.

"William," she called.

There was no reply and as it was only a small garden really, just a strip between the house and the small cliff, she soon realised William was not in it. The gate was still bolted high up on this side so he could not have gone out to the front. A stab of fear -- he must have escaped from the back.

Randolph had insisted on a netting fence in order not to block the sea view, but as she could find no gaps in its mesh she was really puzzled. Then she noticed that some of the trees (planted as a windbreak) grew higher than the fence, and beyond, through the rank tangle, something had flattened down the weeds. An elderberry branch lay broken off, the leaves fresh and unwithered. William had obviously climbed over.

A worried Mrs. Paton made an undignified exit over the fence. A few steps and she found herself on top of the cliff. It was not a big cliff -- a crag rather -- from which came the burbling conversation of the nesting fulmars. One swept past her on its stiff pinions.

"William!"

"Mummy!"

It was a weak cry, in a voice she hardly recognised as William's, but it rang out with an urgency, a directness that she had never heard before. She craned out to see over the gravelly edge.

William lay on a rock shelf near the bottom, thirty feet down perhaps, and was obviously badly hurt.

"Come, please," the boy called.

"One minute, darling," she cried, and fled for help through the captive garden and into the street.

****

They were very kind to her at the hospital but the doctor explained there was nothing they could have done. He had not suffered.

"Did he say anything? she asked.

"Well, yes, but not much, and it hardly made any sense really. 'Tell Mummy they wanted me to fly'."

Mrs. Paton cried when she returned home, wept with the stored misery of five long years, and cried with the despair that would never know, now.

"Mummy! Come please," had not sounded like the cry of a wounded bird. It had been a real boy calling out.

She would never, ever, know......

GLASGOW BOOK SHOP

I don't visit Glasgow very often; yesterday's visit will suffice for the next few months, I hope. Glaswegians are marvellous people and it is one of the most human of cities. My mother's mother came from somewhere off the Great Western Road, so I'm biased: I like Glasgow.

But I'm basically a Fifer and have to live where the North Sea can periodically flatten the poor garden and topple my home-built 'Cat' over in the Forth. I can lie in bed and watch Inchkeith's light flicker its time pattern on the wall.

It was to give a lecture to the Langbank Sailing Club that I'd wangled a day off to go to Glasgow. After some business in the city center I was driving out when a book and junk shop caught my attention. I've a good library of sea books and try never to pass anything by, especialy old junk shops. I remember finding -- no, never mind -- nautical book chat is like sailors' tales.....

I swung off the road to find somewhere to park. A football, followed by a chatter of young Pakistani kids, had me stopping sharply. There were curses from the car behind, curses from me -- and what I took to be curses in return. I pulled in where a notice said 'No Barking'. Behind it, on the wall, there were chalked assorted obscenities. At the bottom of the hill the new ring road was stalking on its concrete legs, kicking down old buildings and tenements, their windows smashed into dirty jigsaws, old mouldings perched or fallen in the clearances. There was a background of piping voices, of sparrows' chatter, of distant traffic. A hot and grimy Glasgow evening.

I went down past a school. A priest was kicking a ball about behind the high wire cage of the playground. A traffic warden waved me across.

"It's a braw day," he greeted.

The shop was like a derelict barge left by the tide. Rubble car parks or teeming streets of cars surrounded its old rotting structure. A solitary wedge of building, shuttered and boarded, empty -- except for this vent from which goods were spilling out onto the pavement in wild disorder. There were three cases of books against the wall, so stepping over a pile of crockery and an evil-smelling pram, I scanned the volumes quickly. Nothing, so I went inside.

It was not always easy to see the books for the items piled up in front of them or dangling from nails on the shelves. There were acres of books really if you could squeeze down the crowded corridors. In just such a place I'd found a 'Slocum' beautifully bound in leather -- and paid for the leather, not the contents.

There was a back room from which came the sound of several voices dominated by a thick, husky female's.

"Tak yir books ben," I was told by the dusty-suited man busy carting in the goods, load by load. "Whit a bloody life," he added. "Every bloody day tae cairt them bloody oot and then cairt them bloody ben."

"Aye, it's a bloody shame," I sympathised, and went ben.

Another room full of books and chests and cabinets and drawers, muskets and spears, was crowded with a group of people, dominated by a dame with extraordinary red hair and an extraordinary deep, filing voice. She was extraordinarily inebriated.

My entry was not even noticed. I was bewildered enough to just stand in this annexe to Babel.

An American woman in a grey cloth suit and rakish hat was prodding a fleshy youth in his fleshiest parts.

"What I say is that Jesus Christ was a mighty fine person. Otherwise how could his influence have lasted all these years? You can't deny that now, can ya? Is that not enough?"

"I don't think so" the youth began, to be interrupted by

Madam.

"These latter day saints are all the same; talk, talk. You canna tell him anything, my dear. Noo, try some of ma guid tobaccy. Dutch. You dinna smoke a pipe? Well, bugger you then for a blasted Yankee. What ah say is this. Never, ever, wid ah buy a German car like yon Volkswagen or Mercedes or Renault...."

Another man attempted to interrupt, and correct. It was like a sandbag in the Nile.

"If it's no effing German it should be wi a name like yon. Think what Hitler did to us Jews, then; I'm no a practising Jew but I'm loyal to some things."

"Christ demands more than just a casual nod. He was a bit more than a man just."

"Ah, shut up, you. Whit de ye think this is? This pipe willnae draw. Hae ye got a match, Eck? Stop rummaging aboot in ma drawers. Naebody gangs through mae drawers. Will ye look at that? He just does whit he likes. Never buys onything either...."

"Well, when were you last in ma place?"

"Ah wouldna be see deid in Pitlochery. Yir too pricey fur me. Rich Americans is your line. Pardon me, my dear. I ken you're yin, but it's no yir fault. Ye're yin o us. A right decent Jew is worth...."

"But I'm not...."

"Dinna haver. Ye're a Jew if I say you are. Ah dinna want a match. Whit's my damn lighter for, dae ye think? Drunk? Me? But of course. Have ye ever known me else. Eck, come oot of there! He just does whit he likes. It's as weel I ken him."

She suddenly spotted me.

"An wha the deevil are you? I've no seen youse afore? Where are ye frae?"

"Fife."

"I wouldna trust a Fifer. But I like Fife fine. Fife's a braw place. It's right bonny up by Montrose way ah say. Whit dae ye want? Dinna gape at me. Aye, it's flat. Nae heid left." (This of her glass of beer.)

"Can I have these books?" I ventured, placing my seven chosen volumes beside her. They had prices pencilled inside. A bit too much but some I was keen on. There had been others I'd sadly said 'no' to. She plonked them down at her slipper-clad feet.

"Ah havena ma specs the day. An whit are you? A damn student or summit? Ye dinna soon like a Fifer."

"I've lived abroad a lot."

"Whaur? London? Look at me, I've been aw roon the world and where dae I end up? In Glescae, bloody, bloody Glescae. Let that be a lesson tae ye. Sold oot tae the bulldozers. Whit will happen tae ma books? I've twenty thousand, ye ken. I've read every yin. Never sell books. Wullie, ye big haddy, will ye watch hoo ye bash they brasses. An dinna girn at me. If I could rise I'd bloody well melt you."

"Ye'd better haud yir tongue," said a lean lad. "Ye're ower drunk tae be let loose on customers the day."

"These are no jist customers I'll hae ye ken. We were discushin deep matters, were we no, hen?"

"Aye, one pint deep."

"Hen, say, that's a cute expression. Is it a Scottish phrase of endearment?"

"Are ye tryin tae make a fool o me? If so I'll no say anither word to a damn Yankee as long as I live an tae hell wi entente cordiality. Maybe I'm a bitty drunk. Wha's tae look after ma wee books when I'm awa? They say I've got cancer. Havers, its aw havers. Anno domini is ma complaint. Anno domini helped oot wi ma daily pinta. Mind, today its been a bit mair but then we've got veesitors from Americy. An Fife. Your're a rum Fifer you are. Can you no buy ony mair stuff?"

"Maybe I can't afford any more."

"Weel, let's keek at what you've got."

She picked up my books one at a time, screwed up her eyes, looked at me, sniffed, giggled and quoted what seemed to be random prices. "Ten bob", "Five bob". These quotes bore no relation to prices marked on the book. Some doubled in price and I just mutely shook my head. Others I equally nodded in bewilderment as she virtually threw them away. I suppose it balanced out but to a collector it was agony. We ended with two piles. There was nothing wrong with her arithmetic, drunk or sober.

"Twa quid tae ye, laddie. Na. Na. Dinna gie the money tae me. Ah canna bide this new money. Wullie, work the till fur me like a good lad. It's a converted machine but I canna understan it at aw. A fiver, eh? A fiver frae a Fifer? Ah should hae charged ye mair. Weel, awa ben there where my best books are. Fancy stuff, ye ken."

I went through wondering what I'd find. Religion? Or rare editions? Pornography, perhaps? It was very anti-climax; just dull Victorian, dusty in every sense. Probably untouched for years and possibly only valuable for an expert. I browsed and took a copy of a MacGregor Rob Roy canoe epic. (I could risk fifty pence at the most for it's worth two pounds.)

She was still rasping forth as I went through.

"Ah bet he's some government snooper. Fifer my fit! Oh, hello, son! Ye've found summit? Aye, its a braw book. Twa quid tae ye."

"Two quid!" I echoed.

"Like it or lump it."

"I'll lump it, thank you."

"Nae need tae thank me. Never trust a German or a toon council is whit ah say. Weel, Fifer, are ye going tae staun aw day?"

She handed me an ill-wrapped parcel and I stomped out. The pavement was clear. The sad man who had laboriously taken everything in was standing at the door.

"She's a bloody, drunken, bloody...." he tailed off. "She didna tak tae ye?"

"I don't think so."

"Ah weel. She daesna tak tae me an I've been merrit tae her twenty taw bloody years. Cheeri-bye."

I went off to lecture. It took an effort to concentrate -- but driving home I had a chance to recall the bookshop; chuckled at the memory. Tonight I untied my parcel after tea, ready for a lazy evening's enjoyment.

Not one book in the parcel had been picked by me. I'd never set eyes on them before.

THE BOY ON THE ROCK

Callum stood poised on the rock for a long time. The sun was warm and his golden skin tickled with the drying sea water. He stood as a thousand other boys have done on their thousand secret places. He often stood there, as, from the rock, he could gaze into the glory of the western sea.

His stance looked out from a tight bay, past skerries that moved the waves of the sea at all times and tides, and away past the big island to the limitless horizon. To the edge of his view the waters were blue, but in the centre, straight out west, the waters were like burnished brass, dazzling the eyes. Callum's face screwed up against the brilliance and beauty. All dreams look to the West.

The rock was his very own -- by right of perpetual usage. Here he gathered mussels at low tide as bait for the fishing; here too he had stabbed a conger eel and felt it writhe and wrap its body up his arm. At high tide he often lay to watch the crabs crawling among the breathing barnacles or the tiny codling that darted about among the wrack and weeds.

The rock divided the bay in two, rising from a blaze of white sand -- made of coral and fragments of shell. Here too were pink cowries which he collected for play-money. He seldom had friends to play with, however, and his brothers were too young to count. The rocky shore shut in the bay and the great rock. It was out of sight of the croft and out of sound of the waterfall that plunged down through the Scots pines and alders towards the shore, half hidden among the heather-topped boulders and rocks.

He was at home on the hill, Callum. Next year his father would really take him out, for he too wanted to be a keeper. He did not enjoy killing, for he loved animals, but it did not raise issues in his mind. The deer had to be controlled, and if people were willing to spend a fortune on a day's stalking that was their affair. If it were not for that there would be nothing else to keep life clinging to that harsh coast. Not that he regarded it as harsh.

Callum loved to stand on the rock in a wild autumn gale. The waves would come surging over the skerries and foam through the mouth of the bay, like live creatures. How often he had perched on the rock, well wrapped up in oilskins, his knuckles white and numb with cold and the effort of holding against the hurricane. Sometimes he would catch a wave full in the face and retreat spluttering and insulted. It was a game, and he gloried in it with the pure abandon of youth.

Even better was when he came of an evening in the summer to swim in the warm waters, diving like a bird off his rocky stance. It was only later that the magic of that repeated moment came to mean so much. On one typical evening it was almost the last fling of youth had he known it. He remembered it so clearly: the lift of his heels from the sharp caress of the barnacled rock, the dazzle of the sun in his eyes and the ageless moment suspended in the air, before his naked body was swallowed up in the grasp of the green depths.

******

Down he dived until he could see the weeds and sand and starfish. He rolled like a seal so the bubbles flew about, and lazily, slowly, arched back to break the silvered surface. He emerged laughing and swam for the shore. He stranded himself in the shallows and let the waves break and wash about his body. Then with a cry like a wounded sea-bird be sprang to his feet and sprinted along the white sands. He climbed up the rock and, almost dry, pulled on his shirt and shorts, jumped down and slowly wended his way home by the back path which came out by the kennels. He was not to return there as a boy again.

There were grim faces when he reached home. It was something about war. He had heard of Hitler, of course, but he had no idea if it could or would affect his home. Two weeks later his father left, and six months later he was dead.

Callum and his brothers and mother went to live with relatives in Glasgow after that, and he grew up among the tenements to the south of the river. He went to the 'Tech' and did well enough to settle in a good job and get married. All through those rough years the memory of home in the far north-west never dimmed. In the awkward years of adolescence it had been his secret retreat and in National Service (when sweating the years through in Aden) it had always been the cottage by the bay that he had looked to as home, a doubly-secret place as he had never been back. As a student, too, when money had been tight and the grind hard, it had encouraged him. It gathered to itself almost a sacredness -- perhaps because it had been so swift and searing in purity, beauty and freedom, and ever since there had been so much that was petty, sordid and ugly.

Adulthood had an even dullness to it and the memory always produced a sense of guilt that he was such a bound creature, travelling every day to the same office on the same Underground with the same company, the same friends, conversations and habits. He hated the numb normality of his city life.

******

Affluence had recently made Callum mobile, and he and his wife Cynthia drove north for the brief two weeks' annual holiday. He had a secret plan to visit the scene of his childhood, but even his wife did not realise quite what a pilgrimage it was. They twisted up the road by Loch Lomond in the rain, but two days later, when they had passed Inverness, it had cleared and the following days shone fair. They took the new road by Shieldaig, and Beinn Alligin shone like a jewel above an early morning mist to welcome them to the land of youth. Many hours later he walked almost hesitantly down the hill path towards the bay. The evening sun tumbled its light down the slope before him and the sea vanished into a haze in the golden west.

He had left his wife at the clachan as she had thought it 'quaint' and wanted to buy a Shetland cardigan and write postcards to everybody.

He hesitated a second. What if the cottage were a ruin -- unlived in all these years? He skirted it by the back path and noticed the kennel railings were rusty and paintless. He took the back path so he could suddenly come on the rock in the bay.

It was a balmy evening and Callum took off his shoes to go barefoot as he had as a boy. After stubbing a toe and stepping on a thistle, he put his shoes back on. He mopped the sweat off his brow. He had to go through a hole below a boulder and he found it a tight fit. He put one foot in the burn, too, and narrowly missed sitting down in it. For the first time in his life he almost desired normality. In perspiring frustration he questioned the sanity of this ridiculous visit.

"Thank goodness, there's the last corner."

Once round it the rock would be in full sight against the Western sea. In spite of everything he felt his heart beating quicker. A score of years was a long time in any man's days and dreams. Callum smiled at his adventure, and rounded the corner.

He stopped dead.

A boy stood poised on the rock. He stood with his face screwed up against the brilliance of the sun-bright sea; the silver shimmer of the waves reflected the light so it rimmed the lithe figure with gold. Callum plainly heard a laugh as the boy lifted on to his toes and flung back the wet hair from his brow. He dived and his naked body was swallowed by restless glitter.

******

Cynthia was on the phone to mother; she had been speaking for a good twenty minutes.

".....Yes........Yes. It really was a lovely trip......heavenly! It's the most lovely country. Callum? Oh, he was in his glory. But you know he can be infuriating. He dragged me all the way to goodness knows where and then wouldn't tell me a thing about what he'd been doing.

"I don't know, I wouldn't go any farther than the shops. He didn't even pay any attention to the cardigan I bought. Cost him the earth, too! He came back looking as if he'd seen a ghost or something.... not a word. He can be trying, but he is such a dear really...."

She went on for a good quarter of an hour more (it was a local call). She had plenty of time. Callum was sitting happily on the underground travelling from Buchanan Street to Kinning Park, his brief-case on his knees and the evening paper open at the sports page.

It had been a good day at the office.

THE MOVING FINGER

Aït Aissa Ali had been trained as a watch-repairer, *horlogier* as his identity card had it on the obverse side, but like all Moroccans he kept a weather eye open for any business that might shimmer on any horizon. The fatalistic *Insh' Allah* with which the whole future is wrapped still allows plenty of scope for human initiative. After all, whatever happens is already written. It was written that Karl that day drove his Range Rover into Taroudant's Gazelle d'Or, one of the most exclusive hotels in the country, and, next day, on the Place Tamaklouk, it was written that he met Ali.

The *place* was the great meeting point for the city, a rough square with a solitary palm, parked *camionettes*, the CTM and SATAS bus stations, several hotels and mosque towers and a spread of outside cafes. Here businessmen sat to make their deals in civilised fashion, here tourists sat and stared (and were stared at), here the touts and guides hung about in hope of something, someone, happening to put a few dirhams in their empty pockets. Here sat Karl sipping a *café cassis* at a table under one of the umbrellas that kept off the knifing sun of the south. His plastic-slatted chair creaked under his large, restless frame. He was not really one for sitting still. He hadn't built up a big, successful company by relaxing over coffees in desert cities. Big-bodied, big-bearded, he looked the formidable figure he was in his business world. Only strict doctor's orders had sent him for a week's lazy holiday in Morocco. His idea of 'lazy' was to hire a Range Rover and cover as much of the country as he could. He drove as he worked, hard and direct. Most traffic let him have the tarred strip when passing. Oncoming traffic was not a call for Karl playing chicken. He took deference as expected. Deals always went his way. He did the writing.

Ali had been sitting in a corner smoking a *Casa Sport* and watching this figure. He took his time and his study was accurate enough that, when he strolled over, he addressed Karl in German. His opening could equally-well have been made in English, French or Spanish. Ali was as precise and careful with languages as he was working with the delicate tools of his trade.

"Good morning, sir" he greeted, diffidently, a smile lighting up his delicate features. Like many country-bred youths he looked almost frail, with skinny frame and soft face, but the body was whip-cord and the mind like a rapier. He quite consciously viewed Karl not just as an opportunity to gain the price of a meal but as an opponent to be fought with in some abstract duel. Personal interplay was just part of life. Were he rich as a king he would still have approached Karl. Karl had all the disadvantages of his inborn and ongoing superiority. Ali, to him was a mere child of the streets, no more remarkable, no more intelligent, than the table at which he sat. His reply to Ali's greeting was little more than a grunt.

"You find the *Gazelle d'Or* congenial, sir?"

That caught Karl off-guard. How the hell did this lad know he was at the *Gazelle d'Or*? Karl looked up, made eye contact -- and was lost from that moment. It was written. Half an hour later Ali was leading Karl to a shop hidden away in the depths of the *souks*.

While enjoying a second coffee with Ali, Karl had suddenly pointed to a tall figure striding past, who was wearing flowing robes and had his head and face bound round with a blue *shen*, a length of thinnest cotton which could be used in many ways to counteract the desert sun, wind, or flying dust. Romance had made much of the Blue Men, Tuareg wanderers who wear the *shen* and whose faces are apt to bear the blue staining of the cloth. Karl was actually seeing one of Taroudant's more elegant hustlers who had never sat on a camel in his life, and whose dress was simply part of a rather effective pantomime. But his *shen* caught Karl's attention.

"That's what I want" he said to Ali. "Can you tell me where

to buy some?''

"Oh, many shops have them.''

"I want forty five,'' Karl added, and Ali, for the first time in years, found someone inside his guard. What on earth could anyone, other than a shop reselling them, ever want with forty five lengths of cotton? Voicing his puzzlement he was not enlightened, but the specific figure was restated unequivocally. Karl wanted forty five *shens*.

Most touristy shops only had two or three hanging up for sale, so this was not an easy commission. Only Mustapha, buried in the covered market area of the *souks* might be able to provide so many. Ali would certainly try. After all, if he gained a commission of just ten dirhams on each *shen* he'd be better off by the monthly wage of a labourer. He explained the situation to Karl.

"Lets's go then!''

So they went in by the bread-sellers and cut through the flea market to the scores of small shops all selling travel goods, trainers, jeans, T shirts and kiddy clothes all with pseudo well-known brand names on them. A few shops still sold the regular slipper-like footwear (*babooches*) and the colourful women's robes (*kaftans*), and these tended to have the odd *shen* hanging at their doors. Mustapha's was more a wholesale shop but no individual customer would be turned away. Ali greeted him in the loquacious fashion of the town and introduced Karl.

"You are welcome, sir, to Taroudant. Please sit down. We have mint tea, yes?''

"I just want.....''

But Ali interrupted. "Certainly Mustapha, mint tea will be most welcome''. When the shopkeeper disappeared for a moment Ali turned and grinned at Karl. "You are not at home now. If you offend Mustapha he will hold out for a very high price. Let me do the bargaining.''

Karl wondered just whose side Ali really would be on, but he was hardly in a position to argue. He knew such items had to be bargained for. Set prices only applied to essentials like foods and fares. Vaguely he recalled his guide book suggesting any initial price should be halved to ensure respect and to be near the real price.

Karl sat on a pile of carpets and Ali on a rickety stool. While Mustapha bustled about producing tea -- in proper fashion rather than just a glass filled with stalks of mint leaves. The ceremony cannot be hurried and is designed to reduce tensions and put everyone at ease. (Ali had suggested the proper ceremony as soon as they arrived, and, in a few words, briefed the shopkeeper about their guest.) Mustapha eventually poured the golden liquid from the bulbous teapot into glasses and handed them to his visitors. He poured from a considerable height so the tea foamed up in the glasses with a cheerful sound.

"Do you know why we do that?"

Karl shook his head as he had just scalded his lips on taking a first sip.

"To those living in desert places the most beautiful sound in the world is running water. Just pouring tea can conjure up pictures of streams tumbling down red banks lined with almond blossom and the air scented with honey."

This was not just the romantic twaddle Karl took it for. After long hours under a desert sun the ceremony of drinking tea takes on almost mystical importance. Ali explained all this.

"The first cup is a taste of heaven. You sip just a little tea and a lot of air so not to be scalded."

He grinned knowingly at Karl, who had relaxed enough that he grinned back. This lad missed nothing. He'd certainly have to watch him during the bargaining -- if they ever got round to it. They got round to it all right, and he, the astute 'King Karl', didn't even notice.

They talked of the desert, of its life-draining sun, of how (unlike in tropical heat) people cover up against the dry, searing heat. Flowing robes insulate. A *shen* protects; it was an essential development, a precious item of protective clothing. Hard to come by. Expensive.

It was only the popping of this word that woke Karl to the realisation that he was already being manipulated. The game had begun and he'd not even heard the starting whistle! Shit! The doctors were obviously right in packing him off for a break. He was slipping.

When it came out he wanted forty five *shens*, the shopkeeper threw up his hands in mock horror.

"I doubt there are so many in the whole *souk*!"

"But Ali said......"

"Unless I have a bale unopened. I deal in bulk, you know. Smaller profits on each item but better gains in the end because of the numbers handled. You know all this. Yours is a bulk order. You will get a very good price compared to elsewhere and you'd take days to buy them a few here, a few there. Let me search."

He disappeared into the back quarters and was gone a long time. Ali poured Karl another glass of mint tea. Shafts of light outside were like sword-thrusts from the bullying sun but it was deliciously cool in the shop. Karl did not find waiting ("doing nothing") oppressive. Normally it would have driven him crazy.

Mustapha had gone out of the back door of his shop and took a fast walk round the Place Tamaklout a couple of times under that hammering sun before returning, brow beaded with sweat, to carry in a bundle that had been sitting to hand all the while.

"After much searching I think I have found a parcel of *shens*." He fumbled and wheezed over untying the knots so Karl wanted to scream out "Let me!". (He didn't want to be the cause of an old shopkeeper having a heart attack!) At last the wrapping fell back to reveal the blue brightness of many *shens*. They all stared in silence, scarce breathing.

It was only then the direct bargaining began. Mustapha explained most stalls or shops would demand 180 dirhams ("You can check if you like") but he, because it was a bulk order, would generously knock off 50 dirhams on each. They were Karl's at 130 dirhams each. In the end, Karl fought this down to 100 dirhams and if this was ten dirhams short of the envisaged "half the initial cost", well, he was prepared to be generous. He had had an entertaining morning. Three hours after he had sat down for a *cafe cassis* on the *place* he came out again to its blinding sun, following Ali, who carried a large package and walked with his mind far away up the beautiful Medlawa valley where his forty five times twenty (not ten!) dirhams commission would keep him in ease for the next three weeks. Everybody was happy.

An hour or two later Karl was anything but happy. He might sign cheques for millions of marks, but every jot and tittle went through his computer brain. He had stopped at several shops in the *souks* and they had suggested prices of 170 to 190 dirhams initially. Mustapha had spoken truly. Mustapha had also said that the dye of all *shens* was apt to come out a little when damped by sweat (hence the "Blue Men") but his were of best quality cotton and the dye would barely run even if the *shens* were immersed in water.

"Try it if you like" he had urged, which, for most people, would have been a guarantee that they did *not* do so. Karl did. Back in his suite at the Gazelle d'Or he filled the bidet in his bathroom with warm water and threw in a couple of *shens*. When he came back from lunch on the terrace he found the water looked like ink. He was furious.

Mustapha had also said "If you are not happy at all, just return goods. Full refund guaranteed always." Karl drove into Taroudant to return the goods.

An hour later he and a somewhat glum Ali sat on the *place* over *orange pressé* drinks. Scowling Karl had no *shens* and Ali's spring visit to the hills had shimmered off into oblivion. The oppressive afternoon heat bore down on them unmercifully. Karl had to be in Agidir for his return flight that evening. It rankled that he had failed to buy his *shens*. Admittedly it was a small failure but it had taken a whole morning and a company executive's salary for a morning's work is hardly in the same price range as forty five *shens*. It rankled.

Had Karl noticed he would have seen a sudden change in Ali's expression. A hint of a smile suddenly lit the young man's face. His curved fingers began to beat out a rhythm on the denim stretched tight over his knees. Suddenly he turned to Karl.

"How long have you got?"

"An hour at the most. My bags are packed, ready to pick up on the way out. Why?"

"Maybe there is one last chance."

"Thanks, Ali, but you've been embarrassed enough. And your day wasted. Would you let me give you 100 dirhams -- as a present. Please."

Ali thought to himself "Half a weeks's salary is better than none," -- but he was suddenly seeing blossom time in the Medlawa in focus again. The game was not over. Nothing had been written -- yet.

"Listen Karl! I know one other shop, on the other side of the *souks*, which might have *shens* enough for you. He is such a miser he hates selling and tends to stockpile all manner of goods. Let me try there. And being old goods his stock could be of better quality *shens*."

Karl admired pertinacity, believing this one of his own great virtues (his associates grudgingly admitted it was, too) and, well, he might just get his *shens* and so round-off his Morocco holiday on a happy note, after all. He patted the straining figure beside him.

"Off you go, boy!"

Half an hour later Ali returned and as he wove through the sprawl of chairs towards Karl the latter knew it was going to work after all. Ali's body language proclaimed success even before he grinned at Karl.

"O.K. He has enough. Old. Good. You want to see?"

Karl leapt up and once more plunged after Ali into the shadowy maze of the *souks*. It took ten minutes to reach the dusty shop. Ali smiled to himself as he noticed Karl consult his watch as they entered Aziz's shop.

Aziz was fat and glum-looking and barely spoke at all. Neither did Karl for that matter. Ali poured out a spate of words, though, arguing and pleading, gesturing wildly at the unenthusiastic shopkeeper. Karl looked at his watch again. Two sets of eyes noted this. Ali turned to Karl, exasperated.

"I tell him everything. He agree. Now he say he will only sell for 130 dirham, not 100 dirham. He is rascal." He turned on the shopkeeper with a torrent of Berber which hardly needed translating. Aziz looked back with a bland, rather smug look on his face. Curses just ran off him, Karl could see. He laid his hand on Ali's arm.

"Offer him 110 dirhams."

"La!" Aziz spat before Ali could even speak.

It was Karl's turn to curse but he looked at his watch as he did so.

"OK. The bastard wins. But they must not run like the other ones."

Aziz stood up and went through to the back premises. After what felt ages to the impatient Karl, he returned with a bucket of water. He walked over to a corner and pulled out (seemingly at random) one of many cylinders of newspaper, blew dust off it, and unwrapped a *shen*. He plunged this into the bucket, kneading it in his puffy hands. Karl almost pushed him out of the way when he paused. The water had barely changed colour.

"OK, I'll take them."

Forty five rolls of *shens* were rapidly parcelled up. Karl only had wads of five 200 dirham notes (the largest denomination available) so, nobody having change of course, he had to hand over 6,000 dirhams, 150 more than the price. Never mind. Everybody was happy.

In the comfort of his first class seat as the Frankfurt flight soared over the snowy Atlas mountains he looked back with the same sort of weary feelings he'd known following a hectic take-over bid. He seemed to have expended the same amount of energy buying his simple lengths of cotton. Ali was nice, though. A good boy. He'd even tried to refuse the 200 dirhams Karl had forced onto him for all his help. And then he had given Karl an emotional hug and a peck on each cheek. Karl pressed the button to summon the steward. He had earned a drink.

Below the starboard wingtip the said Ali was pouring mint tea into the glasses of Mustapha, Aziz and himself. He poured from a great height.

"Do you know what it sounds like?"

The grinning Aziz knew his cousin Ali's joke already. His father's sister's son and he had been partners in many a scam over the years. Germans, especially, were so easy.

"Well?" queried Musatapha.

"It sounds like a man peeing down a hole in the floor when he has drunk too much. When Mr. Karl has had his fill of beer he will go to the plane toilet and make this sound." He lifted the pot so the water arced down from several feet up. Not a drop spilt. They chuckled.

"Do you two not sometimes feel ashamed?" Mustapha queried.

Aziz shot back "It was written" and their going over the day's doings was raised, for a while, to the heady level of a theological dissertation. Aziz concluded "It was written. We did not bring the foolish German to Taroudant." Known as 'Smiler' to his friends his had been the hardest part to play. His scowling visage before Karl had been largely due to suppressed laughter.

"Cousin Ali can now afford his visit to the Medlawa. And no doubt cousin Ayicha will be blushing and happy at his coming." He tousled Ali's hair affectionately. Then they did their sums.

Mustapha showed his receipts for the consignment of *shens* he'd bought the week before. Even imported from Taiwan they had only cost 15 dirhams each. Ali had promised him 30 dirhams each for the forty five he'd rushed in for that afternoon - plus an equal share of any profits thereafter. The number included one of the *shens* Karl had soaked at the Gazelle d'Or. Ali had bombed round to Aziz thereafter, and they had frantically set up the scene in one of his shops. The *shens* had been rolled up in newspaper and then dust from the yard was liberally sprinkled over all. The already-soaked *shen* was given another good rinse so little further dye came out. It was spread in the hot sun to dry while Ali went off to fetch Karl. Everything went off just as planned.

They had 6,000 dirhams. Less the 1,350 Ali had agreed to pay Mustapha, that was 4,650 dirhams to share between the three of them. 1,550 dirhams each of clear profit. Not a bad mark-up on goods which had cost 675 dirhams. (To put it all in proportion, a worker earns about 30 dirhams a day.) Ali would certainly enjoy his holiday in the high Medlawa.

He kept quiet about the 200 dirhams Karl had given him as a 'thank you'. After all, that was not part of the scheme, but a direct present. It was not a matter of conscience at all. It was written. Everybody was happy.

TAIT'S TOMB

We were daft on riding in those days. Both wee Hugh and I haunted the stables down at the Lower Mains, willing, unpaid slaves, our arms kept busy with currycomb or stable broom, brush or polish.

Mrs. Kirkton, who owned and ran the stables, had a heart of gold, we decided. She was young and pretty, far removed from the cartoonist's tweeds and brawn of the 'horsey-type'; that she was a widow with a young family to bring up, that our help was a relief (however slight) -- these were things of which we were completely ignorant. Ours was a short-sighted, purely selfish indulgence: a love of the beast, of the free rhythm, of the sensual smell of life. The ultimate joy was to walk some tiny "beginner" home to the Back Road or the Old Town (nice and far away) and then come riding back, myself mounted on Silver, my best love, Hugh on Colombo.

Mrs. Kirkton sometimes spoilt us thoroughly. I am sure she 'fixed it' that two girls staying at the Castle Hotel in Glendowan had to have the horses taken to them rather than *vice versa* - so she took Silver and another horse up in the box before going on to Perth, and we were left to bring them back through the hills. The road along Glenever Reservoir is grassy and level but every now and then little inlets made sharp bends. We took it at a gallop. An unforgettable experience. We came through the pass towards evening and as we passed above Castle Gloum the whole of the Dowan valley was a golden glitter of sunstreaks. Even chatterbox Hugh was silenced by the view.

If that evening is recalled for its 'fierce joy of living', another a little later was to give us what Hughie called 'the shivers'. To this day I cannot pass Tait's Tomb on the way to Tilly without the memory tingling the hairs on the back of my neck.

Mrs. Kirkton loved horses and loved kids, so she never knew when to stop. Constantly we would still be going over the jumps in Trigger's Field at dusk: we were forever clopping down Bridge Street with the echoes and moonlight playing tricks among the square-cut buildings. The time comes back now as a single, singing summer; if it rained, or some pony was intractable, some horse ill, if tiny tots cried and tempers ran tight, then these are forgotten.

Often, too, when tuition was over, we would go out on the Tilly Road, for Mrs. Kirkton had rented fields there and was also helping to look after a herd of Shetland ponies which Lord Haverton had built up. I often wonder what became of them, for while I was doing National Service out in Kenya, I heard Lord Haverton had died and the estate had been sold. On return I found Haverton Castle had been razed and the Pony Meadows were under the plough. But in their midst, walled like a keep, Tait's Tomb still stood, a ghostly gesture reaching back to those days of innocence.

One night Hugh and I had been to the 'Bughouse' as we called the cinema in Tilly. We came out too late for the last bus, which did not worry us, and too late for a chip supper, which did concern us, and set us grumbling up past the cemetery on the three miles home. It must have been early summer for at the top of the brae we clambered over the wall to visit the sandpit to see if the sand-martins had returned. We then wended on along the snaking road: lined on one side by the ruler of railway line and crowded in upon the other by tall trees which danced in a hot, dry storm.

It was repulsively hot, the heavy breath of the gasping west wheezing at our backs and bullying us along. There was not a chance of rain. The scarp of the Ochils ran blackly back into the weirdly-lit west. Over Sheardale Brae the moon glowered, as though hot inside and swelling, ready to burst over the tepid night. We were reduced to a panting silence, ill at ease in this mysterious menace of nature unnatural.

The trees rubbed their limbs against each other, swayed their tops and rippled their foliage so that the world was full of moaning and groaning, of sighing and whispering, of rustling and hustling -- of some huge primeval imminence that never materialised. We stole furtively down the middle of the road; stamping on each cat's eye for its soft-solid reality.

About half way home the road makes a big sweep left round the Pony Meadows while the railway goes straight on. The woods were thicker on the left and at the back of them somewhere lay Haverton Castle, a building of stark sandstone towers. This half circle of fields had always been used for the Haverton ponies and, in the middle, lay the walled circle of the graveyard known as Tait's Tomb.

This was the family burial place of the Havertons' predecessors; a jungle compound full of brambles and adolescent-looking trees, here and there monstrous marble urns and slabs, obelisks and angels; gentry all, with an admiral and an archbishop among the forgotten beneath the rash of nettles. It was a place all boys and girls shunned and into which few adults would bother to penetrate.

As wee Hughie and I came to the opening out of the Pony Meadows the circle of wall rose starkly from the white moonfields. We stopped together. In that moment the wind died; silence struck swift and deep.

And fear struck. In an instant it had us by the heart. It is not imagination to describe shivers up one's spine. We both shook! I recall Hugh's knuckles white as he gripped my bare arm. My chest hurt with a heaviness like lead, my stomach muscles seemed tied in hanks; Neither of us could even open our mouths for we would have screamed and screamed for relief.

Wee Hugh swears that in that sudden silence he clearly saw the tops of the trees in Tait's Tomb in movement -- though the great beeches besides us surged up in cathedral silence. I saw nothing; but Tait's Tomb to me also was the centre of our terror. The moon-washed mausoleum seemed utterly satanic -- rather I should imagine as Alloway Kirk appeared to Tam O' Shanter as "in a bleeze''. We did not people it with warlocks and witches. It was utterly still; if Hughie's trees moved, it was motion without noise. Yet the fear rooted us to the road as firmly as the beeches were rooted in the bluebell banks beside us.

We stood I suppose mere seconds before I managed to gasp "Run!'' and we shot off. We ran in terror -- for remember the road made a great sweep -- convinced that something from the Tomb was tearing across the fields to cut us off. We felt that if only we could pass that silent, unblinking wall of stone we would be safe, secure from its unknown horror.

The silence was the greatest terror of all.

We ran and ran; God, how we ran!

Eventually we turned the far-away bend and sped past a house, and the spell broke. Then we gasped and wrenched our driven bodies. We lay on the ground, rolling in emotion and howling with the mad laughter of release. But we were silent and uncommunicative as we walked the last mile home.

The next night we and some others were going over the jumps in Trigger's Field. Mrs. Kirkton had been along at Lord Haverton's all evening but her car drew up at last. "Tim! Hugh!'' she cried, without getting out.

We trotted over. Her face, turned to ours, bore the marks of hard work and worry. "Sorry to be late, lads. Can you just pack up now, please.''

Our faces fell, but orders were orders. I was about to nudge Silver when she added "You know the Pony Meadows. I've been there all day. The ponyman says that two of the mares dropped their foals last night and they were all wild and frightened this morning. Something awful must have happened last night to scare them.''

As we did not answer she added "See you at the Mains,'' and drove off.

I ran my hand down Silver's neck, feeling the comforting strength there. Yet last night even the Shelties had gone mad out by Tait's Tomb; the terror had not been ours alone.

To this day I cannot pass the spot at ease; more than a quarter of a century though it has been since the night when boys -- and ponies -- ran inexplicably in terror from Tait's Tomb.

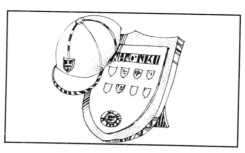

THE CROSS

To enter for the Cross-Country at all one had to undertake six practice runs during the previous weeks. Then on the great Saturday, the first Saturday in May, the dedicated line up on the First Hockey Pitch, for triplicate departures: Juniors, Intermediates and Seniors. The awkward and the athletic alike, *en masse*, in house-colour kaleidoscope, vanish through the Old Gates for the Burnside and Easter Mains. Parents and former pupils, staff -- and the few infirm or ashamed -- hang in clusters, chatting, remembering, barely hearing the Games Master's commentary as he gathered information from the various check points run by the C.C.F Signals Section. I, too, do my remembering.

Of races long ago. Of my first. Of the dramatic second. Of the endless practices. The public school disciplining of a twelve year old.

I was lucky not to be a Boarder, of course. Their practices were so often dreadfully organised by big bullying House Captains or the Sports Captains. I could do mine at my own pleasure and pace, with friends or the dog Jock. Not infrequently bird-nesting or rabbit-hunting or the like played havoc with times and training aspect, but nobody expected me to do more than gain the odd point; so long as I reported to my uninterested House Captain that another run had been faithfully followed, life went on in its peaceful way.

It was an interesting enough route, even the short four-mile Junior version. From the Mains you went down almost to the River Dowan, then up by Hatton's Wood to Stevenson's and then Stoddart's Farms -- quite a pech -- before jarring down the Back Road and in again by the Prep School Gate. The winner did it in about twenty minutes; for his dedication he gained ten points for his house, the second received seven, the third five, then all those within five minutes of the winner three points, within ten minutes, two points, and if completing the course, one point. so everyone who could staggered round.

I had managed two dutiful points in the first year.

The dog Jock had often been a companion on the practice rounds. He was a typical boy's dog: a devoted fox terrier -- a terror to all cats and postmen but loyal as could be. He was as kenspeckle a figure as myself, for we seldom roamed apart. We knew every wood and burn, every den and hillside. We lived at the east end of the town, too, so he was well-known to farmers Stoddart and Stevenson.

Both these gentlemen were elders in St. Mungo's, our church, where grandfather was also an elder; both had families at school, though a bit younger than myself and all the mothers of course were Women's Guild members; so through many connections we all knew each other as folk do in a fairly small and closely-knit community.

I had completed a couple of rounds of Junior Cross practice in my second year when the Games Master drew me aside after P.T.

"Oh, Beattie, it's been been brought to my notice you do your Cross practices with a dog. It will have to stop. Understand?"

As I did not understand I returned, poor fool:"Why, sir?"

The reply was a slap and a "You impertinent brat. Because you're told!"

"But I want to know, sir...."

Five minutes later I went off to Latin with tingling hands, punished for insubordination -- the art of not knowing when to keep one's mouth shut. Good training no doubt. It certainly helped me in later years to wiggle through National Service with my conduct described as 'exemplary' -- and my contribution nil. The gods are always right.

Latin was mostly taken up in a baffled search for sanity somewhere in the recent incident. I had been called 'cheeky' and other incomprehensible words describing unknown attributes. I just was not. It was a completely unfair belting. 'Brought to his notice'.

Who? For crying out loud -- no-one objected the previous year. Or why? Everyone knew old Jock. It was just inconceivable that either Mr. Stevenson or Mr. Stoddart could have complained: Jock and I roamed their land at will, even in the middle of lambing when we loved to 'help'. They could hardly have complained. Or could they? One's disillusionment at the conduct of adult examples came fast. Raeburn the P.T. bloke, for instance, had always been O.K. -- yet loses his head at a simple 'Why?' -- hits me -- belts me. It was souring, illogical, so very unfair. Why could he not say why he was imposing a silly ban? At any time I could take the dog round that same course (for it's a natural walk) and no comment would follow, but because of this sacred season it was suddenly a crime, the mere questioning of which gained not helpful explanations but blows and accusations of being cheeky. It was hopeless and the day passed in misery. No more Crosses for me, thank you.

However, the gods were soon at it again. The House Captain this time. Cornwallis-Smith Senior (later to be thrown out of University and now running a garage, I believe).

"Beattie, you sod, this is the week before the Cross and you've only done two practices."

"So? I'm not interested in your bloody Cross."

"Oh, you're not, are you? Well, you'll fit in the rest of your runs this week -- and be running on Saturday -- or I'll give you the beating of your life. The House needs even your miserable point. So crawl round or else...."

I was left to gaze after the retreating seventeen-year-old. My feelings welled up in tears as I walked home. I changed into shorts and plimsols. Jock watched, tail wagging in expectation.

"No, you mutt, you're banned."

Bark! Bark!

"No!"

The tail stopped wagging, slowly, unbelievingly.

"Oh, Jock, you don't understand either."

I pulled him onto my lap and roughed him up while hot tears

dropped on my hands.

"I hate them all."

Strange moral compunctions. Nobody ever dreamed of falsely claiming a practice they had not in fact done. Yet what evils had been stirred up to set me off, dogless, round the rainy course that evening. Beatings, threats, hates, fears panted through head and heart as feet squelched the paths or crushed the overwhelming scent of hyacinth into the air among the beech trees.

I ran blindly, in an emotional vacuum.

Mr. Stevenson was standing with his two collies by the byre as I passed the yard.

"Hello, Alistair. Going to be Junior champion on Saturday?"

I forced a wan smile.

"Where's old Jock, your other half?"

"At home," I gasped, and was out of speaking range, glad not to have to explain fully.

So it certainly wasn't farmer Stevenson who had brought Jock to Raeburn's attention. Thank goodness. He was a nice old chap. His dogs were great, too. But why? Why? Why? The whole affair had spoiled a week and now another had started, and it would be full of it, a practice a day, a damned, damned jog, jog, silly, bloody, bloody practice a day.

I toiled up to turn at Stoddart's Farm, Law Hill above, the sweeping view down to the fertile valley below. Mr. Stoddart was our elder and a great friend of grandfather's. They both 'kept a bee' as they always put it. His was mainly a hilly sheep farm, high above town and school and the lusher cow pastures. It was cleaner, brighter air up there. I loved it, and slowed to a walk, letting the balm of the evening's coolness flow over my hot soul.

"Jock ill or something, Alastair?"

It was Mrs. Stoddart.

"No. No. He's -- he's banned from doing Crosses with me."

"Why?"

"I'm not told why. Just because I'm told."

"Sounds damned silly. Are you in a hurry?"

"Not really. As long as I go round the daft course."

"Good. Can you take some daffs from the gate bit for your mother? She wants them for church on Sunday. Save a trip later. They'll keep fine."

"O.K."

"Give her my love."

"Cheerio."

"Bye, Alastair."

I picked an armful of daffodils and trundled down the Back Road, almost hoping to meet the rat Raeburn. Perhaps he'd take exception to doing practices with bunches of daffodils! It seemed it was just him who objected. I might be no damned good to him, but I knew more than he did about lots of things. I'd show him. The legal minimum. His pound of flesh.

Each evening I dutifully did a run: moodily, with vengeful dedication rather than the old, carefree and careless dandering. I dodged a bit, careful to add to the route rather than cut it, in order to miss the farms. How could I explain to either Stevensons or Stoddarts? *They* asked *me* why the dog was banned! Perhaps as fellow irrational adults they might have been able to explain, but it was all hurtful enough without opening up further avenues of possibly painful misunderstanding. Best avoid the farms, for the week anyway.

Saturday came with all its fuss. Cornwallis-Smith Senior had all our House lined up for a pep talk on the usual twittery Nelson touch of expecting that every man will do his duty *et cetera*. I even gained a personal salvo.

"Good of you to come along, Beattie."

It was wasted sarcasm. I was cold and miserably far away.

We toed the side lines of the first Hockey Pitch for the start. Raeburn raised his gun.

"Ready!"

The bang bounced us forward into our individual paths: ants in our mass yet each so entirely alone. What was *he* thinking. Did *he* hate this farce? What's *he* grinning at? Watch your elbows!

Through the Old Gates -- the Burnside -- the old road to the Easter Mains. Thank goodness it was the last run.

I could see my grandparents' house. Jock would be shut in the kitchen. Probably yapping his complaint.

I thumped on angrily, red vest stretching in the rhythm of deepening breath. Other reds were about, and greens, blues and yellows. 'The honour of the House' Raeburn was for ever preaching. 'House Colours' -- 'School colours' -- the glory of gods like Cornwallis-Smith, braids and badges, caps and cups, medals and medallions, the bribes to justify the system. The knighthoods for forty years' drudgery and forty thousand cups of tea on the desk, all meaningless to Jock's master, running with emotional emptiness. Next year I'll have flu or something. They can have their race. Raeburn. Ra. Ra. Ra.

I grinned at Mr. Stevenson who was standing outside his gate watching. Halfway already.

"Go it, Alastair. You show 'em!"

Show 'em. For days and days I'd been wishing I could.

Then a brainwave. Perhaps I could drop out? Simply wander off up into the hills for the morning? Or go home? Tear that vital one point expected of me into tiny, tiny pieces.

The pull up to Stoddart's was no place for clear thinking. I passed a gaggle of various-coloured runners and realised there were only a handful ahead, including Inglis who had won last year. Possibly due to my private preoccupation, I was completely unpuffed and physically fresh. Suddenly I realised this. There was another way I could show them. I'd win the bloody race!

The thought certainly caused a rush of adrenalin. I immediately tripped over my flipper feet and landed in the mud. I scrambled up again laughing at my madness; but as soon as the rhythm was restarted my feet seemed to bang, bang the message: 'Win! Win! Win! Win!'

Without undue effort I passed the few stragglers who had slipped back from the leaders and tucked in at the rear of the leading knot of four. They looked tense with competitiveness, glancing at each other, planning like chess players as the End Game emerges from a cluttered board. It was almost funny.

They were runners, though, and I was not. I doubted if I could do any dramatic sprint across the playing fields. Inglis was 440 junior champ too. He was edging into the lead already; half a mile from home. I'd have to go *now*. Being used to charging down the braes of the hills, it was *my* ground. I bounded forward down the old Roman road which ran straight and steep into the town. I'd often done so before -- usually in walking boots -- so this was like skipping in comparison.

Halfway down I'd passed all but Inglis. He was in my House, too, but being dedicated and a pet of the Cornwallis-Smiths of the school he was enemy as much as anyone. I drew level with him and a startled eye glanced to see who had come up. That glance cost him the race, I'm sure. Being about the last person he could expect he gave a perfect double-take, staring, and staring again, so his concentration broke and his stride faltered. I went through, pushing as hard as I could.

By the turn in at the Prep School I had a clear fifty yards lead. But starting across that wide open expanse of hockey pitches was my undoing. The sheer enormity of my position horrified me. Ahead lay crowds and cheering: a scene and noise which was abhorrent to a shy youth whom the establishment had already consigned to the limbo of the inept. Prep kids were staring from their groups across the pitches. You could hear the incredulous "It's Beattie!" My resolution faltered. What had I done? Oh, heavens!

And there was no way out. From the far out scattered Prep kids an ever-more solid funnel of spectators drained one towards the finishing tape. I was certain the cheers were for my House rather than me. I glanced back. Inglis was head back and sprinting -- desperately trying to tear back the distance surprise and steepness had lost him. Och, it would be easy just to let him through. Let him face the palaver of prizes and praise.

Suddenly I spotted the House god. Cornwallis-Smith was inside the line with other Captains to spur on their minors. But as I drew towards him I heard his bass trumpet call, "Come on, Inglis!"

If he had hit me it could not have been more unkind. Inglis and I were both in the same House and both far enough ahead that nobody could pass us. It was a fatal dis-service. Poor lad, he was coming on with all he could muster while I had slackened right off.

That call was a goad that jabbed me forward through every thought and feeling in a last blind burst. I passed the tape several strides ahead of Inglis.

'A gallant rally' the local rag was to call it.

We both sprawled on the grass, blown completely.

Cornwallis-Smith came up and shook my hand. "Well run, Beattie. The House is proud of you." I looked at him -- and looked and looked. I could paint his portrait yet as he was that day. My loathing was complete, my reply raw silence. He turned to pump Inglis up and down. Others were crossing the line steadily. The loudspeaker kept up its raucous commentary above the din of voices and sporadic cheers. The Seniors drifted off for their starting places. The Inters would be half way round their Cross already. The fuss had not been too bad. Raeburn and the Headmaster came over.

"Well, Beattie, your concentrated training seems to have worked wonders."

The Head smiled and almost whispered (so I alone heard) "There are races and races, boy, and reasons and reasons eh?"

Ah, well, it was all a long, long time ago. I stand here remembering it all so clearly. Somewhere up there my son will be passing Stoddart's Farm. (the Stoddart who was a Prep kid in my day), ready for the jarring descent of the Back Road. It is his first race.

BLYTH'S FREEDOM BUGGY

Blyth Drummond was a bit of a madman on the bike. Everyone swore he would kill himself one day. The speed he went. Cornering like that in the rain. A menace to other road users. However, as he was banned from driving for ever-lengthening spells, folk began to bring the odds down a bit. He might have a twenty-first birthday, after all.

He was a nice enough lad, aye cheery and willing to give a hand to anyone in the street, a good tenor voice in the pub, too. There was never a charge of drunken driving. He did not hold with that. It was just the speed he always had to be going at. He'd give you the willies, and if you called him a daft gowk he'd just grin back and say "It was all under control."

Blyth didn't go and kill himself. It made us all feel darned queer after what we had said. It would have been easy if it *had* been his fault, but it wasn't.

He was bashing along from the Wemyss into Buckhynd, enjoying the bendy road no doubt, when he comes round a corner and there is one of Norrie's tractors in the middle of the road with a trailer full of bales. He swerved out to pass. The road ahead was clear. Then Norrie's blessed collie bitch daunders out from the back of the trailer right into his road.

Och, anybody would have swerved, which at yon speed was fatal. Big Blyth skited right off the road. Norrie was back shutting the gate to the field behind him and hears the dog yelp and a great clatter., He was just in time to see Blyth flying right over the hedge like an old rag doll.

There's quite a brae there down to the railway. It took Norrie some time to reach him for you could not force the hedge (it was hawthorn). He could hear Blyth groaning so knew he was not dead -- but old Norrie near died when he got sight of him.

Well, there it was. Blyth did not kill himself as we all expected -- but there were no more bikes for him. It would be a changed laddie would come out of the Victoria in Kirkcaldy. We all felt that sorry. I mean, it was really nobody's fault. Poor Norrie took it awfully bad, though. Poor mannie.

Aye, and poor Blyth. Weeks before any visitors could see him. I used to go along with his sister whiles. She's such a quiet one, it was Blyth did most of the talking with her. He *seemed* to be right cheery but he must have been down in the dumps many a time over the months. Fancy, just twenty, and knowing it would be a wheelchair for life.

Both legs were off above the knee and he was paralysed too. He had a list of other 'wee' things too: a fractured skull, a broken arm -- any *one* would have done most folk.

It was a great day for the village when he came home. One of the lads cracked "You'll be as big a menace in your chair as you ever were on your bike, Blyth", and if ever a joke backfired, yon one did. You might have guessed with Blyth Drummond -- out to prove himself as good as any lad in the place.

He'd even leave the chair and haul about by his arms. I saw him over a dyke pinching apples, if you please. And that chair! He had a right old honky horn on it and liked nothing better than to wheel up to a couple of old gossips on the pavement without their kenning, then HONK! HONK!

But the thing I really wanted to mind came later, after he'd got the *Freedom Buggy*. Yon was a twenty-first birthday present if ever there was.

That was his name for it, one of those three-wheeler invalid cars. He had the guts out of it and by the time he'd finished tinkering it went like a bomb. You couldn't keep him away from speed -- or anything on wheels. He was a great mechanic. During the day he worked at the Remploy so it was still the poor Wemyss-Buckhynd folk that suffered. Yon thing was never meant to travel at fifty mile an hour.

He had a proper engine in the Buggy too, not one of the 'wee hoovers' as he joked at the Remploy. He used to have them all fooling about in the yard so it was like the dodgems. Maybe they couldn't reverse but they could birl round on the spot like peerie tops. They all painted names on their cars like he'd done.

The '*Freedom Buggy* '. That was just typical. It wasn't an invalid car, just a big toy. He was great for getting fun out of anything. Mind, he was serious about it, too. Freedom was very important to him. He left Remploy after a year, to set up on his own as a mechanic.

One job he did was to repair farmer Dryburgh's milking machine, and he was so wild at its inefficiency he re-designed the whole thing. He worked at that all winter, took out patents and goodness knows what else. A manufacturer agreed to come in -- if Blyth could prove he could sell the goods.

So all the next summer he was never home. Off for days at a time across Fife, travelling around in the *Freedom Buggy*. "The deil and a Fifer are baith hard tae persuade" they say, but our Blyth persuaded more than enough to go over to his method. It was easy and cheap, for you could *convert* most makes. We were as pleased as any to see him making a success of the venture. There was talk that over next winter they'd set up production at Glenrothes New Town. Fancy being Sales Manager and a Director of a company and not yet being twenty four. He was fair buzzing about that back end.

One night his sister was in seeing me, worried like. Blyth hadn't been home for four days and never a word had she heard from him. He was often away for a few days but that was always carefully arranged, and if anything cropped up he gave a telephone call. He liked a good meal when he got in!

Next afternoon we went to the police. They knew him fine, naturally, everybody kens everybody in a village. They tried to find him and you'd think it would be easy enough. He had called at a farm near Tilly (that's Tillicoultry, below the Ochils) five days back and that was the last trace. By the morning of the sixth day we were fearing something awful had happened, like he'd run into Alloa docks or something. Where was the *Freedom Buggy* if it came to that?

His sister was ben having a wee cry when an ambulance drew up at their door. We went fleeting out as you can imagine. Blyth was carried in on a stretcher. Half the village was standing watching.

"Whit's the matter, Blyth? Whit's the matter?" she cried.

"Nothing, lass, that some food won't help. I've not had a bite to eat for five days."

It's a laugh now, but, jings, that *Freedom Buggy* was as near the death of him as the bike had been.

He'd left Tilly and gone up through Coalsnaughton for the Dunfermline road and home, then decided to look in on a farmer at Dollar as well. He could ring from there to say he'd be back later than expected.

Blyth was a great one for wee back roads. Farm tracks were no problem. He even had a long gadget, a sort of 'hand' on a pole, which could unhook gates. He *had* to be independent, do it all himself, so this afternoon he took a wee side road off -- a road he had not been on before. He guessed it would lead down by Sheardale and he'd come out by the Dowan Mill bridge.

It was quiet and cooler in the forest. He just hoped the ruts would not become any deeper or he'd be stuck on his belly on the grass ridge in the middle. He could get out but even he couldn't push the *Buggy*! It was not exactly a short cut to Dollar.

Blyth came out of the forest with the Dowan valley below him and the scarp of the sunny Ochils above. The track was a bit rough but that was all the more fun. He stopped to pick some brambles -- leaning out to the bank beside him. Then he drove on into a sort of cutting and rounded a bend -- to brake hard and stop. A bit of banking had collapsed across the track.

Blyth at once realised how serious the situation was. He could not drive forward. He could not reverse. In stopping he had put his nose between the bank on one side and a big boulder on the other, so he could not turn nor open either door to get out.

He was stuck there *for five days!* With half a flask of coffee and a few biscuits left over from his dinner. Blyth aye makes a joke of it, but it was a long, hot spell like you can get at the back end -- and nippy at night too. It's my guess that he was as near gone then as ever he was. Some *Freedom Buggy*.

It was the police who told us all how he escaped, for not a soul appeared all that time. He ran his battery flat sounding his horn and doing things with his lights. It seems daft that a body could near die of hunger and thirst and heat and cold -- right bang in the middle of Scotland.

They said he kept his head OK, for after five days he had the gumption to try a right risky idea. Remember, he could not get out of the *Buggy*.

The bank above was thick with bracken and brambles on the west side and the wood was not far back from it. The wind was easterly -- conditions were just right for a fire!

Blyth crumpled up a ball of newspaper and set a match to it and chucked it out and up as far it he could. The bank went up in a blaze all right -- and he just hoped it wouldn't burn back his way. If it got at the petrol tank.....

An hour later he heard voices, and was discovered. In pretty good shape, all things considered. But that's our Blyth Drummond. We're all proud of Blyth Drummond in the village now.

THIRTY YEARS

Thirty years is a long time, especially when you have counted the monotonous years day by day, telling them as beads of despair, looking to a sky without skylarks, hearing the sea only in the hollow harbours of a pulsing skull.

I left this place with the curses sizzling like tide-tossed shingle. I came back as unrecognised as a cloud, unsubstantial as a gull-cry in the night, the nut-brown local laddie now pale as a November haar, the booming foghorn on the island an eerie echo of my soul.

The harbour seemed much the same, its red blocks rounded by sea years, the same old boats tugging at weed-draped ropes: *Hope, Out In Time, Alison, Northern Star.* How many generations have worked their worn timbers? The men I saw were the men I remember -- but they couldn't be, for thirty years must have swept the old men of my youth away. These were my contemporaries, and I knew them not. Their rocky reality could no more grasp my presence than their nets could hold a jellyfish. I stared at their hard reality (gnarled hands working with skill) while they, if they even spared a glance, looked through me, seeing nothing, seeing nobody. My hands have no skill. Thirty years I have laboured but in thirty years I have acquired no skill. There is no skill to be found in this sack of bones they deem to call a free man.

I walked along the sands past the harbour, leaving erratic prints on the firm band by the black tideline. I recognised many of the shells but their names had gone. I picked up delicate shell butterflies and blew the sand from them. I rinsed them in a pool I dug at the edge of the sea and stared at them for long minutes. I remembered doing just that as a boy, and now, as then, a puff of wind from the island blew them from my palm, and I wept. Thirty years without walking a sandy bay can feel like eternity. I took off my shoes and socks and waded into the chill green sea. I must have stood, still as a heron, for half an hour and only came back to reality as the rising water started to splash my trousers. A minute for every year that was; but could any penance regain the innocence of a child on an empty bay? The empty bay is inside me and my body is made of sand.

I headed off up the steep High Street. There were plenty of changes after thirty years yet it was the old familiar names of shops that caught my eye. People's voices bore a familiar accent but were so loud and brash. They scared me. Not in decades have I looked people in the face or spoken above a whisper. There is no need to shout in the great loneliness. Some of the busy matrons with their shopping bags smiled at me. They smiled at everybody. As I used to do. Everyone knew everyone in those days. The village was part of one's being. It still was, obviously, but I was an outsider in it. Some of these people must have known me at school, would actually remember a pulled pigtail or a frog placed in a trembling palm. All would remember why I went away. Three hundred years would not erase that memory, but, thirty years on, they might not even remember my name. Certainly nobody recognised me. They smiled at the white-haired stranger and went about their daily round. God, the sheer assurance of their daily round: so sure because it was chosen and loved and lived. My thirty years had been imposed and worn and had killed. It wasn't me who returned but some ghost I did not know. They took thirty years to kill me and then were cruel enough to offer a resurrection.

At the top end of the High Street the church and the school still faced each other, institutions which tended to 'top and tail' most of the population. The great chestnut trees surrounding the church seemed just the same. Thirty years is not much in the life of a tree. My feet faltered as I approached. There just could be a teacher who would recognise me, and I would prefer to stay a ghost. But to pass on the other side? *She* might be lying among the trim, grass-plattered gravestones. I don't know. I never heard. Nobody, in all those years, brought me news of the old place. My parents might have, but, before they had recovered from the shock, their car crashed off the Glen Road and they were killed. That was put down to me, too, I was told. Bad news always got through. After thirty years in a sewer the blind rats cannot smell of roses.

The notice board beside the church steps offered the gilded name of a stranger. Not that the minister of my youth was other than a stranger. He never made any contact. Sinners, mild, theoretical sinners were fine, excellent material for pulpit rhetoric, but I froze them all with shivering reality. Odd, it was me, who could hardly look anyone in the face; then, it was as if I had the evil eye. Mary Magdalene found a Christ but I am left, one of the Gadarene swine, but lame, and longing for the cliff edge of oblivion. *She* had a beginning and an end. A history. A brief life. I have an immortality apart: a long life, all of which runs beyond death, a long life which is all chained in that one day long ago. That day is forever my death. There is no Amen.

Two children were scuffing the leaves, hunting for the spiked balls that hide treasured conkers. In a couple of weeks they will be strung and launched into battle. What faith in such tiny, finite things. The boys were aware of my staring and pranced off round the churchyard wall, giving me the fingers sign and laughing. I would have done the same at their age, no doubt. I picked up a big conker, shiny and soft with newness, and rubbed the bloom from it. How often I had planted a conker and watched the birth of a new tree. Someone, somewhere, always took my chestnut trees when they were a foot or two high. The village must be full of trees I have grown. They'll be sturdy young trees by now, their origins unknown (or all too known) and they will burst out sticky buds and candle flowers long after the end of the memories that exploded thirty years ago. Tears wet the conker as I rubbed it in my hands. A tree outlasts generations of men -- and never sins. Why was I not born a tree?

Why was I born at all? Why could I not have died thirty years ago?

At the foot of the Glen Road the lane on the right ends at what was our home. I never saw it again -- and dare not, now. They found me, days later, away over the hills, weak and wandering. I never saw my home again. It had lost something of being a secure place even then. All young men have to break the bonds and the bounds of family. I never meant to break hearts as well. I didn't kill them. They did not kill themselves on my account. That was the cruelest lie of all. We squabbled. What teenager doesn't? When I heard they had been killed I cried my eyes out. *They* treated me more for that than the other thing, I believe. After all, I don't remember what happened, up there, I only know what *they* all described, over and over, till I knew it by rote, knew the utterly vile thing I was. Then *they* all left me alone, which was bliss. But, after thirty years, the brief bliss had turned to a lingering hell. Maybe the first tears in thirty years will water a new growth or freshen a new death.

In the Glen an old pine had been felled by a gale (long before the war) and from its wounded side a mere branch sprang up to become a tree in its own right. We kids marvelled at it. Trees are so strong. Trees are not subjected to *them*, not questioned to death, trees are not un-made. I threw the conker along the lane and took the Glen path to discover the pine, not just for old curiosity but because the thirty years of eating dust and drinking death had their beginnings in that place. My return was ordained. *They* saw to that. And God have mercy on my soul.

The Glen had been out of bounds to kids after the war. The paths and bridges had fallen into decay. It was a marvellous secret place. I remember how as cadets, we were sent on navigational exercises over the hills, and because I knew sea and hills so well we worked a fiddle that was never found out. Instead of sweltering over the hills we made for The Glen and the big pool below the Scar. There, in the dappled depth, we swam away the afternoon while, periodically, I would squat by the walkie-talkie and report our mythical movements to the silly officer (a science teacher) back at base. We would dry off our nakedness in the sun and run all the way back to school so as to arrive looking hot and tired. We would then be packed off to the showers!

All that was a long time ago, but I remember. It swims into focus so clearly now. Maybe because I have not looked out from my death for thirty years. But it was because of *her* that I had to seek the old pine. It was our trysting place.

I have not seen it so clearly since we were there together. Thirty years of painful painting has failed to obliterate our fresco of young love. Why did it go so terribly wrong? It was ordained that I return. Maybe, up there, I could find rebirth. Or maybe real death. I had thought they were different, death and life, but I have been shrouded in both for thirty years and am so tired, so very tired and old and spent. I would welcome another death. Or another life.

I found the old pine: a mature tree now with a peculiar double bend at ground level. How often we sat on that horizontal trunk and talked the sun down in the west. First love has so much to say. (Since then I have spoken fewer words in thirty years than in three hours with *her*.) Hidden by dusty bracken a hollow ran along beside the tree. I kicked off my shoes before walking into it. No doubt *they* would read great significance into this, but *they* will never know. This was the spot where we trysted. Here we discovered our great love, here bared hearts and souls and bodies together. Of course I put off my shoes from so holy a place. I worshipped and could hardly come away. The joy I was seeing through a thirty years tunnel was so sharply real. I have not known such heart-clarity for thirty years. The scene was jewel-clear, like a Pre-Raphaelite painting. Me. And *her.*

And then it was as if some vandal had come along, spray-painting graffiti on the vision. The scene vanished in confusion and fire. I trembled and, through the black smoke in my scorched mind, saw the horror. I had gone to the tryst and found her -- and another. He fled, but not far in such nakedness, and when he returned it was to find all our clothes scattered about the hollow, the rival vanished and the TEENAGER RAPED AND MURDERED IN SECRET DELL as the papers would burst it on the world. *They* told me all this later. *They* kept telling me. Over and over. But I had fled through the bounds of reality by then. Now I can only remember *her* smiling and reaching up to me from the hollow by the twisted pine. The rest never happened. How could it happen? I was dead. I've been dead these thirty dreadful years. And thirty years is a long time when you're dead. Or alive.

ROBBERY, THE SAFE WAY

Mr. Smart took two years to decide on a life of crime and, once launched, his career lasted just two months. He ended by being fined a sum greater than the sum he'd stolen, and he received a six-month sentence which rather took the foam out of his mattress. Well-planned 'jobs' just did not have any come-backs.

Mr. Smart needed money and money. He had dabbled in some wild ideas which had merely singed his savings and restricted his pseudo middle-class life style. He ran the village's only taxi, and there was simply no way he could see how he could earn more or expand the business. He hated being called out at any time of the day or night. He hated most of all his seemingly affluent passengers, though they never knew it. "I'd never be able to afford a taxi" he thought blackly. He hated passing forty (years, that is, not miles per hour). There was plenty of money around. Didn't he see it when handbags were opened and his fare paid? "Keep the change" often interrupted his thoughts of grabbing the capital.

After two years of dithering, which he considered had been years of hard thought, he had his theories clear. Big jobs were out. He wanted to work alone, finding scope where others had overlooked opportunities. Being quite unphysical there was no way he could attack people directly. He would use brain, not brawn, working everything out in advance so there would be no slips at the time, or afterwards. It was the blueprint imagined by every criminal that ever was, but, coming from such an innocent, Bill Smart thought he was being original.

Over many years he had made periodic visits to the Safeways supermarket in the nearby county town. They stocked exotic items like pitta bread or courgettes which the village grocer never offered. Bachelor Bill had gastronomic pretensions, yearnings exacerbated by so often dropping customers off at posh restaurants which he couldn't afford. He could just imagine rolling up at *Le Maroc*, helping a fur-clad partner out of someone else's taxi, marching in, able, and willing, to pay cash for anything and everything fancy fell on.

Dreams like that were in his head as the Safeways assistant at the cash desk rang up his modest total. He handed over a fiver and the girl slapped it under the spring in a compartment crammed with notes. Next to it were brown tenners and strangely coloured notes which could only be twenties. Mr. Smart swallowed a mouthful of saliva as he took his change and watched his goods being banged into a plastic bag. There must have been several hundred pounds lying bare as a tart's tits a mere arm's length away. His criminal career began, quite knowingly, as he made his exit with a pot of pâté, half a melon and some garlic sausage. They were out of pitta bread.

It took two months hard to work out a safe way of robbing the till. At first he envisaged a straight hold-up. If he took the desk nearest the exit doors he could grab the loot and be away before anyone could move. But he had no gun nor could he see himself using one even if he could find such a thing; and perhaps the girls had buttons they could press which would raise an alarm.

But he could get a toy gun easily enough from the Woopee Toyshop at the other end of the High Street. Wait till there was no queue. Tell the girl not to yell or move, showing the gun only from under his jacket, taking the notes, walking calmly to the door.....

Once outside running would attract attention. There was no near lane to dodge into. There would hardly be time to walk anywhere before a noisy pursuit would start. He'd need more time to work out how to counteract yelling shop assistants.

He then had his flash of genius. He'd go out, yes, but instead of running away he'd turn back into the entrance door. The last place they'd look for a fleeing thief was in the store. He'd buy something ('with the money just nicked') and go out the back entrance to the car park. The girl would see him coming in, of course, which rather ended that idea. Or did it? Could he not corrupt the girl? Turn her into an accomplice?

Which is why it took all of two months to set up. But he got there in the end. Big, blonde Beryl, 'Beryl the Boobs' as her mates called her, would be going off at 5pm on the chosen Friday when she'd be on the till nearest the door. At ten to five the supervisor began collecting money from all the positions, otherwise, being the busiest period and late-opening, the money would soon be overflowing the till. "Becomes a security risk" Beryl grinned. "We're supposed to close the till before helping customers clear their groceries. We can't look at the till and the groceries at the same time like. But mostly we just half-push the till drawer. The next customer's usually stuck behind a trolley anyway. Sure, there's an alarm button. Lights up in the office and rings in the watchman's place. Yes, I'll have another, Billy boy. But not so much lemonade in it this time...."

He'd come to quite like Beryl during their planning sessions in a quiet corner of the *Admiral's Arms*, even if it cost a few quid and the pub was fifteen miles away from the town. He felt quietly patronising, too. She had been just the right choice. No fuss. Quite a nice girl really. Taxi drivers knew how to judge people.

"What if I'd gone and reported you?"

"Oh, I'd deny it all and you'd just look daft. There's absolutely no proof. Nothing exists except in our minds. Can't fail."

For £50 and the promise of a posh dinner in the city Beryl had agreed to his plans.

At 4.35 he would see Beryl put up a POSITION CLOSED sign. At 4.40 he would go up to Beryl's position with his basket of groceries but it would be groceries *and* money from the till which would go into the bag. He would calmly walk to the exit, go through, then immediately in again at the neighbouring entrance. Only then would Beryl press her alarm button under the desk and rush to the door, raising a good old hue and cry. She'd be good at that he could see.

"But how do I explain not pressing the button earlier?"

"Last thing in the basket will be tomatoes. I'll drop them onto the floor inside the counter. You can then say you were picking them up when the gun was turned on you. You couldn't reach the button as your seat was in the way. Nobody will doubt you. There'll be tomatoes all over the floor and the till will be empty. No doubt they'll search you but even *your* cleavage can't hide several handfuls of notes." He grinned at her.

"You've got it all sussed out, haven't you Bill? And what if I hold out for a better cut? Fifty quid ain't much when you'll get maybe four hundred."

"Then I'll just get someone else in another supermarket."

"OK! OK! I was just teasing....."

It went like clockwork. Beryl put up her POSITION CLOSED sign and two customers girned off to look for the shortest queue. Bill came up and laid down his basket. Beryl rang up the prices, opened the till, quite casually pulled out all the notes and shoved them in a carrier bag along with the groceries. Bill tipped tomatoes onto the floor behind the counter and walked towards the door. He went through both sets of doors into the street, grinned at the fresh blast of autumn air, then turned round to go in again. He pushed against the neighbouring door and, through it, saw Beryl, sitting on her stool with a huge red smile on her face. His cry of "Silly bitch! Get on with it!" was cut short as he banged up against the glass of the inner door. He pushed again. The door did not open.

Then he pushed the outer half. Nothing happened. He was trapped.

****

Beryl was making the most of telling her tale. The rest of the assistants sat in the rest-room, wide-eyed and wide-mouthed.

"Oh, he was a scream. Just like a goldfish in a tank. Pushing here, pushing there, scrabbling and yelling, then hammering on the door at me, then his face changing as the security staff came up on both sides. Feel quite sorry for him in some ways. Had three good nights out in the pubs with him. If he'd only been more generous, who knows.....?"

"When he asked about the alarm button I only told him about the light going on in the office and the bell in security. I forgot it would also lock the doors. So when he only offered me £50 and I remembered the doors would lock I made me own plans. Trapped him beautifully, didn't I? So, Saturday night, have your blokes waiting. It's the chinky, pictures and pub for everyone. There's £200 to spend."

Stories travel as stories do, and one of prisoner Smart's mates rather enjoyed putting Bill right on Beryl the Boob's double cross.

"You were too greedy, see. Girls get £100 reward for anything they do to help get thieves convicted. You didn't just go off with a tin of baked beans, though, did you? So she got £200 reward. Saved the store from an armed desperado, she did.''

"But I wasn't armed! Not even with a toy gun."

"All she said was you stuck something in her back when she was bent down. Could have been a sawn-off carrot for all anyone knew. You could do with someone like that, mate. Smart chick. Very smart,'' and he laughed unduly at the adjective he'd inadvertently used.

****

A year later SMART TAXIS were all over the town. And they really were smart. Quite different. Used for every special occasion. And such a nice girl when you phoned. "Good evening. Beryl Smart here. What can we do for you, madam?" was a bit different from the normal "Aye, what you want?" And Bill thrilled every time he heard her voice on the speaker. "Hello, Mr. Smart. Mr. Brewster is off to the city. When you have dropped your gentleman can you please go to 23 Primrose Street. A Mr. and Mrs. Houston for a 7.30 date at *Le Maroc*. Then I'll expect you home, dear. There's a nice supper and the pitta bread will be piping hot, just as you like it.''

CASUALTY

I tell you, it ain't fair! Life ain't bleedin fair! What does a seven-year-old kid know about it, eh? Bleedin fat girls with big tits. They were the ones that were queer. What they muckin about with kiddies for when they were strong enough to be 'Digging For Victory' or working making bombs or somit? You just could not have been any more innocent than we were. I mean to say: seven-year-old!

Never knew me dad. Livin where we did he was a sailor like as not. There were enough of them, even during the bleedin Blitz. But Jerry got me mum. I never seed her again once the siren went. Probably not quick enough out of bed. It was the old kitchen table saved me, even if one end of it collapsed and fetched me one on the 'ead. Next thing I knew they was pullin me out in me sleeping bag and a fireman was saying "Bastards! Bastards! Another fucking kid." But I wasn't dead and I managed to croak out "Mummy" so the fireman near dropped me in his surprise. *Picture Post* had me picture sitting starin out me sleeping bag like a baby kangaroo. "Miracle Boy" they called me. Maybe I'd be better if the bastards had got me. It just ain't fair.

Two days later they shoved me on a train full of other lost kids. We were wrapped up in big coats and had just one parcel and our gas masks. They made us try them on and thirty, forty kids, waggling and gaggling in gas masks was queer. We were labelled like bleedin parcels and sent off to God-knows where in Wiltshire. I'd never seen the country before but I can't remember much anyway. We were shell-shocked, I reckon, numb-like.

We were put up in a hall for the beginning. God, I can

remember the stink of it still. Some kids were always pissing themselves or spewing. It was hell. Yet we all tried so hard to please the 'Aunties' who looked after us. Some of the old birds were OK. You could just snuggle up to them and they'd rock you for hours. Sometimes I can remember big, hot, splashy tears landing on me face. No, it was the younger ones we hated -- always trying to 'take us out of ourselves' with walks and games and rowdiness, when all we wanted was to burrow down through our blackness into some quiet place. They even tried to take away me sleeping bag but I yelled blue murder till they gave it back. "Dirty", they called it.

Probably was dirty, too, but it was all I had in the bleedin world. It was one of those standard air raid issue things filled with kapok that looked like dirty cotton wool. Me mum had added a blue edging round the top and down the side where it opened out. It was me haven for more than just them air raids, I'll tell you. When mum was rowing with whoever was staying I'd go and hide in it. No way were they taking it away from me. Such heaven as was left a broken child was nearest in that sleeping bag. Then came the awfulest night of all.

The Big Tits were making us play games again. One of them banged away on a piano while we danced about in our sleeping bags. We tried to make it look like we were enjoying it, and maybe some stronger kids did, but most of us just kept falling down or being silly. When the music got higher and higher we had to be ready, when it stopped, to yell and cheer and hold our arms up full length, making ourselves as high as possible. When the music growled lower and lower we had to get ready to collapse on the floor and make ourselves as flat as possible and hiss like snakes. It was a bleedin silly game. But most of the big tits were silly bitches, if nothing worse.

Next time the music went up, up, and stopped I reached up real high to please them, holding the corners of me sleeping bag out like a big sail. But the elastic must have gone on me pants for me belly and everything else popped out in full view. You'd think all those grown-ups had never seen a prick before. Bleedin fuss! They yelled I was disgusting and I was packed off to bed without me cocoa.

I lay in the corner snivelling and wondering what I was supposed to have done. I could hear them going on about it. "Exhibitionist....Just think of him when he grows up....Little pervert." I didn't know what the words meant -- then. They were all wrong. I was just a kid. I wasn't anything like that. I wasn't.

But I am now.

BY YON BONNIE BANKS

Bill wiped his nose with the dishcloth.

"Stop that, ye filthy midden!"

Bill sighed, inaudibly, and shifted the clothes-horse so as to reach the table

"An tak yir paws affy ma washin."

Bill sat without rancour. It *was* Sunday morning after all. For the rest of the week he was out of the house before Aggie stirred. He just quietly said, "Aw, haud yir wheest and gies ma tea."

Aggie grabbed the brown pot off the gas and dumped it on the tacky oilcloth that covered the table. She lifted her piercing voice to bellow through the door.

"If youse twa are no through this meenit you'll get nae breakfast the day." Without altering pitch and with scarce reduction of volume she turned on Bill: "Could you no pit yir shirt on fir a change? Galoshes at the table!"

"I'll pit ma shirt on fir breakfast when you tak yir curlers oot for breakfast."

Aggie's hand went up to her head. Her black hair was churned up in an array of bright plastic curlers. She was twenty eight but the thin pinched face with its long pointed nose made her look older. She had been 'Beaky' as a child and Bill was still apt to call her 'ma wee speug', which was not really such a bad description. She had been sixteen when she married Bill. "Shot-gun weddin?" the gossips queried. "Maybe aye, maybe hooch-aye," was their unsatisfactory conclusion.

It was no great love affair, but rather a tenement tie-up; simply gaining something all girls wanted and most men demanded. They tholed each other, Aggie with her sharp tongue, Bill with his utter ordinariness. Their two boys were hardy as cobblestones, the bairn still in what Bill called the 'snotty stage'. There are miles of such homes along the brown river.

Bill, a year or two older than his wife, also bore the years badly, for the flesh hung on him loosely and large. The hair had receded over his crown. After a night in the *Rob Roy* and a long lie there still clung about him a certain tiredness. He did too much overtime.

You could guess he was a welder. Perhaps it was the tightness of his eyes or the peculiar metallic smell that permeated garments and skin so thoroughly. His fingers were ingrained and his hands were rough. He loved to flex them (a habit which riled Aggie) for he was a skilled craftsman who had been in the 'Rankin and Coventry' for fifteen years. Twice this last year others had been paid off but he did not fear redundacncy. They had both lived in Govan all their lives.

The boys came clattering into the kitchen but fell silent as they sat down to their Sugar Puffs and rolls and, because it was Sunday, bacon and eggs. The room was hazy with the cooking, the smells of frying mingling with that of the drying nappies on the pulley. Aggie handed the twins identical parcels.

''Yir new jeans. Pit them on efter ye've eaten. We're going for a run the day.''

They undid the wrappers which Aggie folded away in the dresser and the boys themselves rolled up the string which she put in a hideous china vase.

Wee Bill turned to Tam and held out the label with a grin. It was not a famous name.

''They're guid enough for youse twa.'' their mother snapped.

The boys ate in silence. They were twelve and a half, small and bright, perhaps as their mother had been once, but to her looks they had added their father's stoicism. They even bottled up their excitement at the prospect of a day's run till they had shoved their plates over to the sink, then, though, in their room they grabbed pillows and walloped each other with excitement.

Wee Bill couldn't find his jeans when wanted and Tam reacted to his accusations of theft by nipping his temptingly bare behind -- so there was a rumpus and poor Bill tore his shirt on a drawer knob and mother leathered both of them. The assembly outside the front close was a tearful one: both boys sniffing and the bairn bawling and struggling.

The boys were safely shoo-ed into the back of the car, an old Morris Bill called 'The Beatle.' That morning there were several alliterative adjectives to go with the B. The Beatle refused to start. Choke in. Choke out. Starter racing. Bill swearing. Several teenagers, after enjoying the spectacle for a while, asked "Dae ye want a shove, mister?" Bill told them to buzz off, only it wasn't 'buzz' and even Aggie rounded on him: "Shut yir bloody mouth. Swearin in front of awbody."

Bill shut his eyes, his knuckles bunched tight and white on the steering wheel. He muttered to himself and tried again and this time the car roared into life. Bill pumped on the accelerator. A neighbour, coming in with the *Sunday Post* commented "Mercy, mun, ye'll hae the guts oot-er." Bill fortunately did not hear. The Beatle bumped off. The bairn immediately started bawling again. Aggie yelled, "Whit de ye think ye've got in yir tank -- a perishin kangaroo?"

Bill did not reply but he was that mad he very nearly went through against the lights at the Cross.

****

"Stop at Balloch, Bill," Aggie demanded. "I've got a splittin heid. I'll get some aspirins."

Bill swung round past the hotel for the shops. The street was busy and the gates were closed for the boat train. He joined the line of cars.

"Can we no see the boats?" wee Bill pleaded.

"Ye'll sit doon this meenit. Yir paw canna see oot the back wi youse twa dancin aboot."

"Aw, Maw......"

"Dinna 'Aw, Maw' me. Can ye no find somewhere to park?"

"Hoo can ah, stuck in this bloody queue?"

"Weel, ye should hae taen the ither road."

"But you wanted aspirins."

"Aye, no a......"

"Maw, can we hae a wafer?"

"No."

"But it's aawfy hot."

"Weel, open the windae."

"Ah canna."

"Whit for no?"

"It's jammed," said Bill. "Here, it's perishin hot. Could you and the bairns no get oot for ices and yir perishin aspirins and I'll drive roon again and pick youse up?"

"Aye, please Maw."

"Ah weel, oot ye get."

The boys tumbled out. Aggie followed.

"Come here noo. I'll hae nae wanderin aff on yir lane."

"Can we no gang tae the bridge and keek at the boats?"

"Ye can dae nae such thing. The gate's shut onywey."

"Aw, Maw...."

"Shut up and stan there while I get the pram oot."

Aggie struggled with the boot. It had jammed too, it seemed.

"Bill, open the bloody boot."

Bill climbed out, presed down as he turned the handle, and pulled the boot open - nae bother at aw. Aggie glowered.

Bill was getting back in when the car behind honked its horn.The gates were opening, the queue stirring to shuddery life. Bill dashed back.

"Come on, Get the bairn. I'll fetch the pram."

Aggie yanked the back door, then swore, for it was the jammed one. She scrabbled in the front. A shoe clattered into the gutter and her posture as she leaned over to pick up the baby brought whistles and comments from lolly-licking loungers on the pavement. Aggie backed out and rounded on them.

"Whit dae ye think ye're gettin at?" she screamed. "If a wisnae a woman I'd give youse sic a walloping yir ain mithers widna ken ye. Ye big louts. Ye muckle...."

The horn blared from behind. Bill was pulling at her arm.

"Aggie, for God's sake!"

She rounded on Bill.

"For God's sake. I'll God's sake ye! Dae ye stan there -- an me bein insulted by a gang o foul-mouthed brats? Here, tak the bairn an I'll deal wi them." She thrust the bundle into Bill's arms. There was a wail of protest.

The lads had wisely nipped inside the nearest shop door, the two boys had gone along to the bridge 'as the gates were open', the other spectators quickly pretended to be studying postcards or their fingers or the sky. Angry Aggie rounded on a vacuum.

The horn behind blared: loud and long.

In two strides Aggie was at the driver's door.

"Wha the blazes dae ye think ye are, ye noisy deevil?"

Bill dragged her away.

"Mind the pram and let me get awa."

She swept off, smacking the offending car's bonnet as she went.

"Sorry mate," Bill said. "But she's in a bit o a temper. It's this bloody heat."

"Aye, it's a fair scorcher. Here, dae ye no work at the 'Rankin and Coventry'?"

"Aye, I'm...."

The car behind that one now blared its horn: solidly, hard, for long, long seconds. They both winced. Then there was silence -- out of which came the summer sound of life by the river. Bill wiped the sweat off his brow.

"Haud oan a minute," he said and strode back to the noise maker. The other jumped out to join his.

Bill leant an elbow insolently on the roof.

"Weel, weel, so you like blawin yir horn, dae ye?"

The other arrived.

"You want a fight, mate?"

The conversation was swamped by a whole cacophony of horns. The queue throbbed like a swarm of bees.

A policeman in shirt sleeves pushed his way through the buzzing spectators.

****

They chose a spot near Rowardenan Youth Hostel for their picnic. The ground under the oak trees was black and soured with over-use, smitten hard with cars and human treading, pitted with pieces of paper and glass. Even the bushes had been broken down. Children paddled in plastic sandals in case they cut a foot on a piece of broken bottle.

Aggie tried to cheer up her dour man.

"Look, there's a canoe oot on the loch."

"Oh aye."

"Is it no bonnie?"

"Aye."

"Och, Bill, yir no even looken."

"Aye."

She spanked him one then lay down, half on the tartan blanket, half on top of him, winding arms around his neck. She slid her head down beside him, rubbing her hair up and down his rough cheek. At last he uncupped his hands, rolled over with her hands held in his, pulling her on top of him.

"Ma wee spaara!"

"Ma Bill. Nae mair sulks."

"Aye; gies another smacker, ye auld bitch."

Tam and Bill burst through the bushes.

"Paw, we've lost wir boat! Come an fetch it back! We canna reach it!"

Bill glared up past Aggie's head.

"Buzz off!"

"But Paw..."

Bill heaved Aggie aside with a muttered "Bugger it!" and went off.

Aggie tossed her hair back, arranged herself in a careless pose, unbuttoned her blouse right down and tried out various preparatory expressions. The heat excited her to unusual desire. Bill might be big and bulky, but he *was* hers. She closed her eyes the better to imagine his embrace, his crushing power that squeezed the breath from her body. One of his hands alone could cover her small breasts. They had had 'some gey coorse courtin' and Aggie quivered at the memory. It had been more give and take in those days; now he was apt to come back from the *Rob Roy* boozed and demanding 'denner in bed'. And Muggins aye fed him. "Dinner's ready, ye muckle sumph," she whispered.

The bushs burst open and Bill stormed back. "Those bloody bairns and their boat! Look at me! Jist wringing. Right up tae ma waist."

"Di ye gan in?"

"Na, ma breeks jist get wet their lane! I fell aff a boulder trying to wrax in the bairns' boat."

"Ye daft galoot!"

"Aye, I could hardly expect sympathy I suppose. Ye're only ma bloody wife, efter aw."

"Dinna fash yirsel. Hang yir breeks on the bushes there beside the bairn's pram -- an come an lie doon again."

With much hopping from foot to foot he struggled out of his wet breeks and tossed them over the pram. He noticed the baby's face was tight with sleep. He looked down on Aggie. Her breasts half peeped from her blouse, 'like the twins peekin roon the door' he thought, 'seein if aw was clear fir mischief'.

He lay down and pulled her close. One hand run under the small breasts, the other cushioned her head; one of hers held him close, the other wiggled down his body feeling the flabby flesh.

There was a scream from the pram.

Aggie girned "See whit's the bloody matter!"

He knelt and looked over, then rose to snatch off his trousers which were were dripping water into the bairn's ear. He threw them down.

Aggie whispered, "Come on, Bill."

"No the noo."

She pulled him backwards off balance, but he broke free to sit up.

"I said no the noo."

"Why no?"

"I'm no in the mood."

Aggie flared.

"No in the mood? But I've to be in the mood when you bloody well want to."

Bill sat scowling in silence.

"Ye're a sulky big bugger."

He laid a conciliatory hand on her arm.

"Dinna touch me! I hate ye! Go away!"

The words whistled out after each other.

Bill heaved himself to his feet. He was about to walk off but remembered he was wearing only a vest and shirt so he yanked at the car door. It was the jammed one and he nearly broke his wrist. He crashed into the front seat. The leather was uncomfortably hot on his seat but he refused to move. There was silence awhile.

"Bill."

"Bill."

"Bill, I'm sorry. Come tae me. Please."

"Nup!"

There was the sound of a car stopping a few yards away. Doors slammed and the wood seemed swamped with jarring laughter and shouts.

Aggie pulled her blouse together and sat up.

****

"It's aboot time we were packin up."

The rug was well covered in crumbs and the dirty dishes still lay uncollected. The rubbish had been thrown under the nearest bush. Bill blew a spiral of smoke into the air and belched. The twins carried on playing paper-stone-scissors. The baby lay fed, quietly gurgling with satisfaction.

"It's aboot time we were....."

"Whit's the hurry?" Bill interrupted.

"The bairns will be late for their beds."

"Weel, it'll no be the first time."

"Och, I jist want tae gang hame."

"Wha's sulking noo?"

"Can we no go?"

"Nup."

The boys winked at each other, then sidled off.

"Ye've nae discipline. They laddies get aff wi murder."

"Aye."

"God, hae ye nothing tae say?"

"Nup. If we gang the noo, *Capella's* willna be open and I'm no goin oot again fir a supper."

"Ach, aw ye care fors yir belly."

Aggie began to collect the things together with exaggerated noise and clatter, then stopped, feeling she was being watched. She looked up, gave a wee cry "Oh, Bill," and stared.

Wacthing them was a tramp.

The tattered clothes were strained over a lean yet immense frame; a huge white beard gave a patriarchal touch to the towering figure.

"Good afternoon. I hope I didn't surprise you?"

The tone was refined --'posh' as Bill later said -- and there was no servility in the stance of the stranger.

"No," said Aggie.

They both stared awhile.

"Could you spare me a scrap to eat? Or a fill of tobacco --

I'm right out I'm afraid.''

It might have been said in some smoke room after a business lunch in the city.

Bill continued to stare. Aggie looked away.

''Piss off!''

Bill flipped his cigarette at the tramp's feet.

The tramp gave a soft sigh and went off.

''Huh,'' snorted Bill. ''Gi'es it back, Aggie.''

But Aggie had her arms full of pokes and thermos flasks.

''Fetch it yirself.''

Bill let the cigarette lie.

''Flaming cheek,'' he remarked a few minutes later. Then he stood up and yelled ''Bill! Tam!''in a tone that brooked no denial. The boys came up from the loch.

''We're going.''

''Och, Paw, must we? Can we no stay a bit mair?''

''Shut up! Both of youse,'' Aggie said, pushing them off the rug and lifting it to shake off the day's debris.

''Change into your shoes and roll yir jeans doon.''

They complied.

Soon the car was twisting along the narrow road by Loch Lomondside, one of a patient line of beasties scrambling to the breathless city. The Johnstones had enjoyed their Sunday out. Back at the picnic spot the tramp sat in the silence, watching the sun jinking down beyond the Luss hills, puffing his free fag and humming the tune that began ''By yon bonnie banks....''

LETTING OFF STEAM

I flipped on the thirteenth. No, it wasn't a Friday or my birthday or onything else. I'm jinxed, no superstitious. It wis just anither hellish day o trying tae find somewhere to park in central Edinburgh in the run up tae the effin Festival, a hot, sticky August day that clung a haze of blue diesel fumes roon the base of the Castle rock like a skirt dropped roon the ankles of a sweaty harlot

What do you mean, poetic? OK, I'll get on wi it. God, I loathe Edinburgh sometimes. Whiles, you just hae to let aff steam. So I phones you.

It aw began on August the first when I had the accident in the car. I mean, I never take it in if I can help it, but I'd a cairpit tae collect frae Phillips, a right bargain as they aye are at auction. Folk pay hunners for rubbish nae half as guid as this wan. For the new glesshoose extension. What them at Morningside wid call a "conservatory" I suppose. Kay has the glesshoose full of cactuses noo. They've actually got braw-coloured floors, showy, just like the wife's claes. She got a right put-doon last week. She was through in Fife an saw a braw frock in a dress shop in Largo. No wey was it going tae fit though. The girl in the shop told Kay that, with the comment that she wis "all bum, belly and breist". At least she could clype on herself and laugh aboot it. Some day I may laugh at whit happened tae me -- when I'm aff ma crutches. I ken I ramble on when I'm excited.

Listen, I'd got ma cairpit - Kay's cairpit -- and had jist pulled oot o South West Thistle Street Lane (would ony ither city in the warld hae a street name like yon?) when a silly bugger cam fleeing doon frae Frederick Street and bashed straight intae me. I know it's a one-way street. So did he. He reversed oot straight awa and went screechin back doon the brae. But I got his number, even if I wis hurt.

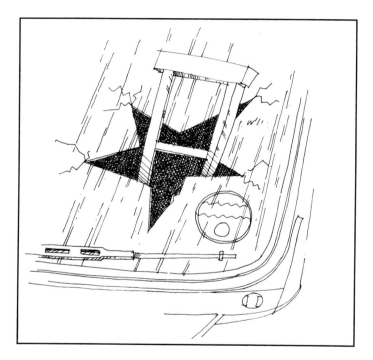

It wis an easy wan tae mind: G582 EFS. That wis *Gee, five ate twa! Evelyn Fairley Somerville*. I dinna ken why five ate twa but you use these connections for minding things, do you no? And Evelyn Fairley Somerville is Kay's maiden name. I reckon I was smart wi that coincidence.

That wis on August the first as I said. I dinna ken hoo mony times since I've said so, or written so -- on polis reports, hospital reports, insurance reports -- you name it. Aye, August the first is no easy forgotten. 11.35 a.m. tae be precise. You'd think I wis the guilty pairty.

There I wis then, wi a stove-in car and masel on crutches. Just a broken leg. "Lucky" they said at the hospital. Lucky! They probably felt let doon. A double amputation might have made August the first something. Whit's anither broken leg here or there?

I'll tell you: it's a right scunner. You try going the messages on crutches. I'm no lightweight tae go birling roon like Tarzan. Ma oxters are richt sair. Onywey, on the thirteenth I had tae gang intae toon. An, if motoring in Edinburgh is hell, the buses come gey near doon tae the same level. They're the pits! The first widna stop for a mere cripple and the next sent me skiting by stairtin aff like a stane oot o a gutty.

I wis staunin on the pavement ootside Thins, gettin ma wits back efter the stress o takin a ride on a city bus, when whit did I see, richt there by me, parked Bold as Bass on the double yelly lines -- Number G582 EFS!

Noo, you ken I'm a peace-loving-like lad, but I'd had ma fill over they last twa weeks. I jist lost it. Flipped. "Extenuating circumstances" they called it later. The car was sittin wi its back tae me but I could see the bugger wis sittin at the wheel. I jist let flee.

A crutch can dae quite a braw demolition job. I'd smashed in his lichts, dunted the back a few times, and stove-in the rear windie before the bloke even reacted. I wis stairtin on the side windaes when he leapt oot, screamin -- only it wisnae a he. It wis a she. A real she she she. I suppose I just gawped. I'll no repeat whit she said, no on the phone -- it wid probably melt.

There's been a richt carfuffle I can tell you. They chairged me. Quite a list. But some o them seemed tae think it a bit of a joke, ye ken. Even *The Scotsman* cam oot wi BACKFIRE ON CRUTCH ASSAULT. Dinna **you** laugh either. It's no funny. Yet.

They gaed me a suspended sentence.

Noo, where wis I?

Aye, well he or she, I was still mad and jist stood there wavin ma crutch and rantin. You could hae heard us in Portobello.

"Whit am I daein?" I yelled back at her. "Whit am I daein? I'm gettin ma ain back for August the first, that's whit I'm daein, when you smashed intae me you, you....."I actually ran oot o words. Me!

"What dae you mean, 'August the first'....Smashed into ye? " she screeched back.

"You know damn weel. Fleein the wrang wey intae Thistle Street an clootin ma car, and puttin me on crutches. That's whit i mean by August the first!"

It wis her gawpin then, She choked oot "I've never bashed onything! I've never bashed ony wan! I only just bought this effin car on August the fourth!"

THE BOY

The first time he ever say the Boy was on the afternoon when he refused to fight Ginger.

It was a hot, grubby, summer day, and a gang of them were chatting and annoying each other outside the Physics Building -- as young teenagers are wont to do after being grilled behind glass for hours listening to a tedious master.

In class his mind had kept straying off to the Snowdrop Valley pool in the Dowan; imagining several friends and himself rushing down through the dappled woods to the coolness of the river. He was still away in his daydream as he stood in that fussing, fractious group outside the labs.

Somehow, like summer lightning, the first point of friction sparked among the gang. Ginger was squaring up to him, eyes blazing, calling him all manner of names which, had his mother heard, would have given her a fit. Others at once were taking up sides, shouting provocation and insults. He was so taken aback and his mind was so far from reality that he just muttered something silly and sidled away. Jeers followed his retreat.

He went down by the Box Wood Hedges, brows wrinkled at the incident, giving it no undue importance, but placidly (he was always so damned placid), wondering what had got into Ginger.

It was then he saw the Boy.

He had that odd feeling of someone being present and a quick glance showed another figure walking parallel with him, the hedge alone separating them. As it was forbidden to cross the hedges he wondered at the fellow's daring; he looked again to see who it could be. It was no-one he knew.

The stranger was a year or two younger than himself, with a prim mouth set disapprovingly. He felt this other Boy was somehow rebuking him, so strode quicker, but the other kept pace. Then there was a sigh (or did he imagine it?) and on looking round the Boy had gone, vanished as if by magic, leaving the shrubbery empty. That was the first appearance of the Boy.

In bed that night as he lay staring into the pale darkness of tired summer he was aware of the Boy again, standing surveying him from the foot of his bed. It was a scrutiny, an inspection, which made him feel almost indecent. "Blast you, I've done nothing!" he swore and covered his head with the sheet, but even beneath the bedclothes he was aware of the Boy watching. Then the feeling slowly faded. He knew the Boy had gone. He pushed the sheet off his face. Pale moonlight illuminated the room. He could see his crumpled clothes, the model aeroplane on the dresser, the prints he had tacked to the corner-cupboard door. That reality was a comfort. He was soon asleep.

He was to see the Boy regularly thereafter, if that is the correct word, for the appearances were to no set pattern; months could go past till he had almost forgotten the Boy, then there he would be again: stiff and often censorious, he was certain, (but not all menacing) -- and always silent. He tried conversation in the beginning, but it was like talking to a puff of smoke or a ghost. Perhaps it was a ghost? Whatever it was, it was his secret; not even his closest pals knew of their friend's weakness. He was never to understand it himself, after all.

He would sometimes stare intently at the other boys and girls in class. Did they have these peculiar visitations? Was this something like the new awareness of one's body and other half-hinted things that really were normal nothings-at-all?

He tried some text books in the Biology Lab. library but psychological phraseology, if nothing else, baffled him. Ultimately he learned to live with it, rather as a classmate managed with just one hand. It was not altogether unpleasant even. Sometimes he almost felt smug about his secret. Perhaps it was his very own? Perhaps all these faces about him really were blank? Yet his pride could not call up his mentor. No Witch of Endor this. The Boy's comings were completely unpredictable.

Sometimes, as with his one-handed classmate it could be embarrassing. They all recalled the young new maths. master who lost his rag at this chap and shouted that he couldn't even count the fingers on his hands. "Ten, you stupid boy. Count them. Hold them up so we can all see. Both hands! Go on! Hold them up...." And the poor kid holding up one hand and a stump.

He had the same from another master, thanks to the Boy.

"You, staring into space. What are you looking at?"

"Nothing, sir."

"Well, if you concentrate on something the way you do on nothing, you'd be an Einstein, lad."

How could any master understand something like the Boy? It was so strange that they all saw nothing. Or did they? Was it all a gigantic hoax? No, that was quite impossible. Hallucination? Well, if it was, it was just too bad. The books did say teenagers had various things like this but grew out of them. Time would rid him of the Boy.

He had called him that from the start. 'Kid' would have been a bit irreverent for something which rather awed him, yet the figure seemed younger than he was, almost a prim, puritan version of himself.

Once he almost gave the Boy away. Some escapade was afoot, and, on being invited to join the fun, he began, "The Boy wouldn't..." only to imagine his sleeve jerked violently and turned to see a scowling Boy shaking his head.

The most disturbing thing was that somehow the boy WAS him. It was like looking into a mirror backwards into time. As he grew, so the Boy grew as well but always appeared that much his junior, his junior yet ever so much wiser, it seemed. One incident was quite weird.

Some of their gang were out overnight on a Scout trip, sleeping in a narrow glen up by the Burn of Darrow, and the Boy appeared persistently in the tent urging him out into the night. He dragged a protesting tent-mate with him and no sooner were they out from its warm comfort than a boulder came thudding down the hillside to sweep the tent and contents into the burn.

He glided through school days with an average success: swimming for the school, playing ultimately for the Second Fifteen and shooting in the CCF without ever making the Bisley team. He was always regarded as a bit of a dreamer by the staff, but his cheerful ways endeared him among his fellows, and he was always a popular figure at dances and social occasions. He was perhaps happiest roaming that calm landscape of hill, glen and valley. Out on the singing heights or deep in the green tree shades he was always content. There he seldom thought of -- or saw -- the Boy, there he learned to love nature and all living things, there he decided to dedicate himself to his fellow men, 'to be on the side of good', as he wrote in an essay on 'Ambition'. He went to Edinburgh as a medical student.

He did surprisingly well there. His detached, adult attitudes, allied to his rather winsome cheerfulness, gave him a personality mature for his years. In his fourth year he fell hopelessly in love with a nurse from Tiree -- Margaret was her name -- but that fell through largely because the Boy had been set against it!

He had bitterly resented the continuing attentions of what he had hoped was childhood fancy. The boy (who was no damned *boy* any longer) appeared as erratically as ever, and the thought of this thorn in the flesh becoming known to his fellow students would make him break into a cold sweat. He thought his studies would rationalise the creature from his subconscious, but it did nothing of the sort. He did find that hard work seemed to keep the Boy away -- and he worked hard -- so it was as well he had an outgoing personality as well, and so moved normally and popularly among his acquaintances.

He grew a beard at one stage, which clearly displeased the Boy. A few weeks later the Boy appeared with a beard, too. He laughed then, exulting in the fact that the Boy could be 'got at', but it was hollow mockery -- rather like trying to make fun of an Archbishop dressed in his glorious yet absurd robes.

Then came the Boy's obvious disapproval of his relationship with Margaret. He could hardly go anywhere or do anything with her but this scowling policeman would be of the party. The cliché about two being company had a vicious ring to it. It drove him to despair, yet sheer fury was tempered by other memories, like that camp by the Darrow Burn and especially by one which had happened more recently.

They were making ready for an operation and he was asked to collect a certain unpronounceable drug. He came back with it and to his horror, beside the eminent surgeon and, like the surgeon, holding out his hand, stood the Boy.

He hesitated fractionally so the great man impatiently wiggled his hand, but the Boy's urgent look was not be denied and into *his* hand he passed the phials -- which immediately smashed to the floor as both he and the surgeon grabbed to save them. Nobody suspected other than a simple if rather careless accident.

"Are you usually so clumsy?"

He flushed deeply as he knelt before them all picking up the piece. One phial was undamaged, but the others were an odorous wet mess. Suddenly he trembled. The smell -- it wasn't what it should be. (Chemistry was his strong point, after all, with the Lawson Prize and so on.) He stood up, holding out his now smelly finger.

"Smell, sir," he said in shocked tones.

Rather condescendingly the other bent to sniff.

"Good God, man, I sent you for--------"

"That's what the labels say, sir."

"Let me see."

The pair of them stooped among the mess.

"I knew something was wrong, sir. I wasn't just being......", and then he shut up. It was best by far to be considered just luckily handless, for he was correct, and the drug had been incorrectly labelled.

"Gentlemen, thanks to this man's clumsy hands but adequate nose, we have certainly avoided a tragedy today. It is something which I would prefer you not to mention beyond these walls. I need hardly point out the serious nature of this mistake which will be thoroughly investigated."

Thinking it over later hardly helped his peace of mind. In all ways the Boy had been correct, often so damnably, morally correct, even to the extent of blatantly interfering to avoid tragedy. How could any romance blossom? His relationship with Margaret grew strained and in the end impossible. He busied himself with his studies, threw himself into the social whirl and even enjoyed the 'War Game' as they cheerfully called the OTC. (The jack boots were marching and their message was becoming all too clear.)

The last years flew by happily. The Boy seemed to be a thing of the past, his House year was nearly over in that summer of 1939. It was almost as if he had been timed for war -- about which he had few illusions (his father still hobbled as the result of the Battle of Loos), and he joined the reality in time to receive the returning wounded off the small boats from Dunkirk.

Eventually he was posted to a big hospital in Ismalia beside the Suez Canal, but three months later his agitating seemed to bear fruit and he travelled west along the shimmering miles of desert to join the more urgent work at the front. Grim, telling months went by.

He had often enough stood in Ismalia at night and watched the silent flickering among the great clouds: lightning without thunder. At the front, it was both, and man-made. The grumble and flicker to the west was the prelude to the day's work, which seemed endless. As he stood there one night, many months later, under the turning chandeliers of stars, he was aware of the Boy standing beside him again. During all the months at the front he had never appeared.

He looked at the Boy and was appalled at how old and tired

his shadow had become. What of himself, then? The Boy looked at him sadly, with blood-shot eyes and drooping lips, inestimably weary.

He smiled at the Boy and reached out a comforting hand -- which met only a bougainvillea-draped pillar supporting the crumbling casualty department building. The stars continued their inexorable swing overhead and the man-made storm flared and died in the gasp of dawn. Soon the sweat would be running down his back as his hands -- his unusually skillful hands -- worked with blood and bone and torn flesh. Not a demon, as his fellow medical officers suggested, but the Boy drove him, through weeks and months of days. His days were raw, red work, and his nights exhaustion below the unquiet skies.

Eventually he was ordered to rest, but before taking the road east to the so-called 'comforts' of Cairo, (to which it looked as if Rommel would soon follow) he went with a unit right to the front line, under the wary eye of an RAMC corporal who came from Glasgow -- Partick way.

It was all confusion and noise.

"Oot tae the *wadi*, sur, we wis telt. An keep yer heid doon."

The *wadi* was a dry valley and along its narrow length a mere thread of motorable road wound below slopes littered with multi-hued boulders and sandy scree. It was a perfect setting for an ambush, and the latest counter-attack had run into just that, suffering heavy casualties. Vehicles were blazing, and, as they entered the *wadi* with the stretcher bearers behind them, an ammo. carrier exploded. It was plain disaster with the weary Jocks caught in the cross-fire from the surrounding slopes. He was certainly seeing the bloody brunt of it. The corporal wasted no time, moving swiftly amid the screaming sounds, hardly stopping his chatter.

"Move this yin, youse twa....Ali, put your bally helmet on, you gowk....na, na, sur, yon yin's as deid as a dodo....hey, sees us a dressing -- ta, sur, no, press there a wee bitty...Tak it easy, laddie, we'll soon hae ye oot o here. Stretcher! Jings, we're poo-in back, sur

-- and no before time if ye ask me. *Dae ye see thaat?* (The last comment as a shell exploded not far from the running figure of a youthful infantryman -- who crumpled, groaning, his body caught in a dozen places by shrapnel.)

He had seen alright. He began to wriggle forward on to the bare *wadi* floor. Another explosion (mortar!) and a shower of gravel fell across his legs. He paused, glanced up, never heard the corporal's "Come back, sur, dinna be daft -- it's bleedin murder oot there!" for his path was blocked by the Boy. The fateful figure was urging him back to the shelter of the boulders. He lowered his head onto his arms, and they almost stuck together with the gritty sweat. Another bang, and a blow cocked up his helmet. They certainly had the range.

The Boy had always been right, so back lay safety, he presumed -- forward, God alone knew. He visualised some of the casualties he had worked on over the last months. He recalled young faces beyond all pain which he had covered up and waved away. Blast it, *he* was only twenty seven -- though he felt as weary as seventy two. He heard the injured lad ahead cry out wordlessly: the language of pain universal, the call as old as the hills.

In raw nature only a few men react to the cry of the injured; but to them the cry is imperative, unavoidable. He began to crawl forward again into the *wadi* -- across the longest twenty yards on earth. The Boy slowly stood aside.

The white band with the red cross probably saved him from near attention. There was no cover anyway. He lay beside the trembling figure, holding his flask to the youngster's lips. The casualty's lower legs were bloody. He would simply have to carry him and take his chance. Even Jerry would hardly shoot down someone so obviously helping the wounded.

He struggled the soldier onto his shoulder and when the youth passed out it made it easier. He began to stagger back to the boulders where the orderlies had a stretcher ready and the corporal was beckoning urgently. A chatter of machine-gun fire made his scalp creep, but it went overhead, aimed at a Bren on the other slope.

There was another explosion -- he was hit -- so painfully as to be meaningless. His left arm felt useless, there was a bloody wound on his face, his side. He fixed all his giddy attention on the stretcher, staggered and fell with his burden into the arms of his lads.

He was not mortally wounded and the youngster he had collected certainly owed his life to him. But a surgeon with one arm? He preferred not to think of the future. Willy-nilly, for him it was long months of pain and rest. He returned to Ismalia -- then Blighty -- and on to a hospital in the Cotswolds where the crow-loud woods themselves and the view of the scented summer miles acted better than all medicines, to both body and soul.

He was lying listening to the evening's quiet whispers when he heard the lilt of an islander's voice. It could have been Margaret from Tiree. The tears pricked behind his lids at the thought. The voice -- and the steps -- stopped by his bed. He heard his name, his pet name, whispered; he opened his eyes. It *was* Margaret!

God, how he had missed her. The Boy had been so very wrong. He was not dead. And here was the one he knew he loved, he loved, he loved! He looked at her strangely-working face then, with his good hand, reached up and pulled her down to him. The Sister gasped and some patients whooped or whistled.

Margaret pushed him back softly, then fled the ward. Sister stiffly scolded. "That is not the way to treat Matron, sir."

He didn't open his eyes, but quietly said, "Oh, no? You just wait and see, lassie."

A minute later he did open his eyes -- and stared about (as much as a bandaged neck allowed). He was correct. There was no Boy. In fact, he had not seen the Boy since the moment he had rejected the warning and crawled out to rescue the wounded lad in *Wadi Oussene.* He was only to see him once more ever again.

That was the day when he and Margaret, his newly-wed, took leave of the hospital. By then the Matron and the Major were immensely popular and the send-off was quite an occasion. The staff were gathered in the hall, and they were all saying farewell, when suddenly he saw the Boy standing back in the alcove under the picture of the king. They stared silently as ever at each other.

The Boy looked tired, but happy, one sleeve pinned and empty, the face scarred and lined; on his breast various impressive ribbons. Slowly the Boy drew himself up and saluted.

He released Margaret's arm and returned the salute. The Boy smiled; the only smile he had ever smiled. The Major passed a hand over his eyes and blinked -- and there, when he looked again, the alcove was empty but for the picture of the king.

Margaret and he went out into the dazzle of sun and snow, noticing happily, as they drove away, the first tight snowdrop pearls under the elm trees.

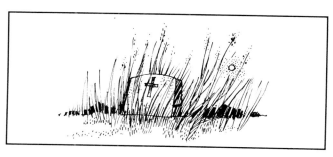

THE SENTRY

He was really so very young -- and so very tired -- for the battle had been remorseless and the issue itself, to his mind, so unimportant and impersonal. Now he half sat, half crouched, like a blue hare on his own heath, and slowly rubbed the spots of blood from his sword hilt. He was a true son of Donald and the blade pleased him. But the battle did not. The general could have used the side glens with better effect. So the independent lad from Glenmore's Alltbeithe judged his superiors, a judgment without bitterness for he served well and only sought to better his skill.

He put the sword at his side where it could quickly be snatched up again. Faintly, among the worn rocks by the gorge, he could hear the noise of the native soldiers, a restless, pulsing noise, like waves heard at a distance on a windy day. They could rejoice wholly for it was their war and their quarrel. If the Auld Alliance had brought him to a nation of friends there were times when that was not enough -- as now -- after this bloody battle. He screwed up his eyes into the west. God, how he looked to the west! With only one hour till sundown the day still blazed in a harsh whiteness that drained all colour from the land and seeped the beauty from the blue sky.

He looked around. The country was poor and dusty, its limestone crags burst like raw ribs from the dry carcass of the land. The river below moved in milky whiteness and the glaciers that fed it showed faintly among the hazy peaks. The grass would carry few stirks, he decided.

There were some bonny flowers: blue ones like stars and whole fields of gold which were neither buttercups nor marshmallows: there were some willows creeping close to the ground and these he knew as he had seen similar when he had crossed a high bealach to avoid Campbell country on his way south to the capital.

And when he thought of that journey he thought of the wherefore and the why.

They had stood off from the Port of Leith on a spring day when the scent of new things filled the air. How green he remembered the fields of the Lothians as they slipped by. How greener he recalled the machair round the crofts of Alltbeithe. Alltbeithe. Home.

And he had exchanged that for this!

He felt sick with disgust, and, of course, with sheer tiredness, though no son of Donald would have admitted to that. (No shame if he had, for he had fought as a true son of his fathers and the prince-general himself had noted his valour.)

He thought of food suddenly as young men will do who have laboured hard all day, and he could look down and see many a smoke rising from the village and from the army encamped round it. The village was small and piled on top of itself, its streets so narrow that four soldiers could scarce march abreast. The roofs were covered with slabs of grey stone and the wide eaves sheltered firewood for the winter. But he could not go down. It was his misfortune to have sentry duty after the day of battle. He would not have known the word 'claustrophobia' but he would have felt it in the cramped and crowded village. His mind swung home again.

There, at the foot of Glenmore, their croft stood alone, the nearest kin two miles off by the shore path by Eilean Ban. Theirs had been but a poor house perhaps, with its hard earth floor and tired thatch; but inside it was cosy. He thought back to the time when he and his brother were bairns and sat before the peat flame while their mother told them tales of Moola in the old days. His father had been taken by the sea when he was seven and life had been hard -- but clean and fair. They had learned to read and write and some luxuries came in with the foreign ships that escaped the King's navy. It had been his father's war then but he had had no father with whom to draw sword. Did he somehow feel he had to justify himself? Did he have to find another prince?

That was the reason he gave out for leaving the croft but his mother, aye, and his brother too, knew there was deeper sorrow in his heart: it was that that clouded his eyes and took the young laughter from his lips, it was that that drove him to stand long hours alone at the end of the beach where the white waves smote on the rock point. His brother was as kind and gentle as possible, for he lay beside him in the bunk and knew his tossing about and sleeplessness each night.

With no surprise then, but with a sinking of the heart, his family heard him one day propose to make his way to foreign parts to soldier as his father might have done. They said nothing of the lie and he departed without knowing the real sorrow he left behind. It had been bad enough -- with the tears in his brother's eyes and his mother desperately holding herself in check until he had gone. He had taken the steep path up through the alders and brambles over the point. The bell heather was budding at his feet as he left the clachan for the long road south.

He had sung a song as he went to cheer up those he left and to stop the floodgates from his own blue eyes. The words bit into his soul now as he gazed unseeing over the dusty plain with its litter of dead men and beasts and shining weapons. God, how he loved the wild westland! -- even in winter when the gales which had taken his father crashed like wild things on the sand and sent the spray flying over the croft land.

Quietly he sang the song again:

The west gat hold o me, mither.
The west gat hold o me, mither.
In the crash o the sea, mither,
In the cream foam flying,
In the ebb-tide lying,
She gat hold o me, mither.

The west gat hold o me, mither.
The west gat hold o me, mither.
In the saugh o the wind, mither,
In the rise o the heather,
In the grey, sad weather,
She gat hold o me, mither.
  The west gat hold o me, mither.
In the crash o the fall, mither,
In the song o the tree, mither,
In the lone bird crying,
In the love dying,
She gat hold o me, mither.

He thought of the bay as it would be in summer's evening. The sun would be setting beyond Mull and the hills would be blue and soft in its light. There would be a shimmer on the waters and as like as not a mountain mist creeping up the ben to make cloud colours. It was aye a gentle sun and a gentle scene -- as gentle as a lover's arms on an evening walk.

With that thought he startled like a stag that scented danger. The real sun glared down on the unhappy man and his agony of soul. Even as he sat the sweat stuck the cloth to his back. He quickly drew the back of his hand over his brow but it was sweat alone he wiped away. The memory could not be so easily effaced. It burst into his soul like the cruel sun, for the years of his exile had altered little and the pain of it had settled deeper. And now, again, willy-nilly, as on many evenings, he sat with eyes turning inwards. He would not have done so normally on duty but he was too tired and a bit fey with the day's battle to be thinking very clearly.

He thought almost in pictures -- always pictures with Morag; Morag, young as himself but to him ageless as a goddess. He had indeed worshipped at her shrine -- and his offering had been rejected.

So he had tried to flee from his disappointment -- only to find it followed after.

An added pain came to him now for he doubted himself, his very manhood; all his courage in battle, his skill on the sea and strength at the plough, what were these compared to this failure, this double failure of losing Morag his desired, and failing to lose the melancholy of his love-lost? He sat a long time staring at the Alps through the grim heat-haze but his soul gazed out painfully from the lands of Alltbeithe.

Suddenly he saw her, or imagined he did, like an angel against the white blaze of sky, moving slowly towards him, silently, almost secretively. He smiled with a vain sort of smile; pleading, asking wordlessly for an acceptance till then denied, for the return of his love that cried from his soul. The figure stood over him.

He never knew what happened next. There was a flash of steel as the enemy's sword went through his breast. His life's blood poured out and gathered with the grains of white sand on the ground.

Then enemy ranks sprang from hiding and went charging down on the resting allies below. To him their war-cries came as the shouts of welcome. He could see Alltbeithe clearly now. The bay circled blue and silver and the dancing of the burn was there. He heard his mother and his brother laughing, and crying in their laughing, at his return.

They stood aside and Morag was there; more beautiful than even he remembered. She was holding out her arms to him. With a smile of content he gave himself into those arms while all the west burst into the song of welcoming.

Donald had come home.

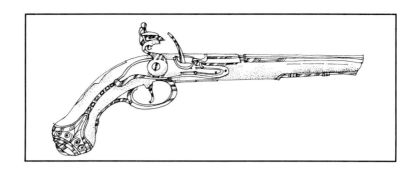

THE ROBBERS

The two garrons clattered down the causey-stanes by the castle approaches. The riders on them were in Highland garb, well wrapped up in their plaids against a snell east wind that was blowing up the links of the Forth. Both were well armed and carried an air of potential menace yet, at the same time, their eyes shot glances out from below bushy brows so it was obvious that they rode warily, but then, most Highlanders did who ventured down into the unfriendly Lowlands towards the middle of the 18th century. One rode for a few minutes with his eyes turned aside to the steep front of the Ochils, as if drinking a last dram of the hills and all they represented. His companion spoke sharply to the dreamer who merely smiled, patted his saddlebags and pointed to the pistols holstered beside them. It was a gesture which did not go unnoticed. A figure on foot who had followed them from the inn turned down a lane to where another man held two horses. The new arrival nodded and both men swung into the saddle and cantered off by a circuitous route that took them out of Stirling and back on the road to Edinburgh. Behind them the two Highlanders took the same road.

The night before that four men had been drinking in the same room. The Highlanders had not been aware of this particularly, for the room was crowded and smoky and noisy with merry-making as any of Stirling's three inns were in early summer. The Highlanders spoke only in Gaelic, which, was besides, the first language of that particular innkeeper. They had chosen that hostelry because it was the one favoured by Highlanders of a certain persuasion and they felt safer among their kind. They drank a dram or two with the landlord, explaining they were bound for Edinburgh to seek their fortune there. Glean Pean was overcrowded and poor. They had sold their boat based on Loch Nevis and one way or another had raised considerable capital with which to try their luck in the city. They were nephews of Macmillan of Glen Pean.

"I am Seumas and this ugly fellow is Iain" one of them said. They were as alike as two peas, and the insult only brought a smile to Iain's sturdy features. They were fresh-faced, likable lads and mine host had made them welcome. He could not stand those with chips on their shoulders.

"Would you try this business, lads?" he queried, nodding to the crowded room.

"No, we fancy trading, perhaps with a shop to begin with. One on the High Street, perhaps, if we can afford it. People are beginning to build town houses. They will need provisioning. We have ties with France. Perhaps we could specialise in wines -- and other better victuals."

"Seumas is good at drinking, you'll notice."

They all smiled. Their host then lowered his voice to ask some questions which were not asked out loud in a town like Stirling where redcoat spies were busy. Thus it was that the two men who were to ride on before them the next day, and who had been eavesdropping from the nook back-to-back with theirs, could no longer hear their words. They looked at each other, shrugged, and went out into the night.

In fact the two Highlanders made it clear they were not too interested either. After all they were in the very process of severing their roots in the west. "We stayed with Locheil, of course, after coming down Loch Arkaig, and he is pessimistic of any rising against the present government. England has the power. France only uses the potential of a Scottish revolt to further her own ends. To annoy England, yes, but not to go to war on our behalf. Locheil even suggested we should set up in London itself. We could be useful eyes and ears there but we must first of all guard our own interests.

All we possess sits in these bags on my lap. Were King James in Whitehall it would be a different matter.'' One way or another they learned quite a bit of information and they promised to keep in touch. The innkeeper lit them to their sleeping chamber and wished them "oidche math''. They lay in a small room, alone, the saddle bags tied by a cord to the waist of Iain while Seumas, pretending to sleep, lay with a hand on his dirk, his pistols, primed below his cast-off jacket beside their bed. They had been warned by everyone about the dishonesty and dangers they might find in the Lowlands and were taking no chances. At a house down off the Castlegait two others sat discussing Seumas and Iain Macmillan and the heavy saddlebag that they kept with them at all times.

Having checked that the Macmillans were leaving for Edinburgh these two galloped and reached Linlithgow by noon. There they underwent a certain metamorphosis. One of them was shaved carefully, washed well, and dressed in clothes which, while reflecting obvious wealth and station, were still practical and without swank. The other dressed to appear as the squire's servant and groom. They then rode back an hour on the Stirling road and waited out of sight till the Highlanders had passed. After ten minutes they galloped east again for a mile, to set the horses breathing hard, then gradually slowed down so they came up on the Highlanders as any travellers might have done. When Iain and Seumas looked round they were relieved to see it was a gentleman who approached, not that they dropped their determined caution. Iain, with the saddle bags, moved beyond Seumas so the stranger came up on the defensive side, so to speak. It was a move which did not go unobserved. Below the newcomer's cheerful greeting were curses that these Highlanders would obviously be canny capons to pluck. The gentleman surprised them by calling out a greeting in Gaelic.

"Gentlemen, you have come from the west?'' A diplomat could not have taken a better opening. "From the lands of Locheil perhaps?'' he added, eying their tartan.

"Iain Macmillan, at your service. And this is my brother

James."

"Good day to you, Iain, and to you Seumas Macmillan. My name is James Grant. Grant of Glentromie which, if you'll pardon my commenting, is too near Ruthven for pleasure, so I have travelled in other lands, travelled and traded, and done well enough, gentlemen, to own a fine house in Edinburgh and mills in Wapping. Ill winds can sometimes blow one good." He smiled in an engaging manner. "And what brings you to the Lowlands? he asked innocently. The brothers exchanged glances. Iain had almost put out a hand to feel the bags were safe at his saddle. God, you had to be careful.

"Oh, we travel on business" Seumas replied rather casually. Grant laughed, and glancing round at his servant, who followed thirty yards behind, said in a lower voice "You do well to be cautious. I was ever too outspoken. But I take you for honest men. You must be out of those clothes this night, though. They will mark you out in the city. I do not want your secrets, if you have any, but it pays not to be an obvious Highland visitor. Have you the English?

"Oh, yes," Seumas answered, swopping into that tongue. "We have been well educated, both at home and -- elsewhere." He had hesitated to say France but the pause was obviously as clear for Grant laughed outright.

"Your English had hardly the accents of Edinburgh. It might be better if it had." He frowned, then smiled again so his handsome face lit up. "Just listen to me. My English is neutral. I can make it sing like your own when I want, or roll like a merchant's speech by the Tyne, or screech with the ugly sounds of London. It pays, gentlemen, it pays."

The brothers could not help but warm to their casual companion. He was a Highlander as well, that was a bond at once (even if he spoke Speyside Gaelic) and he had obviously done what they were attempting, and he was obviously a warm handsome character, who, dash it all, couldn't be ten years older than they were. They eyed his sleek mare and its expensive trappings, the rich accoutrements, Grant's tasteful clothes and white linen. Could they be as he was, a decade hence? They relaxed and began to enjoy their companionable ride to Linlithgow.

Jamie Grant knew the best inn and led them to it. After drinking and refreshing themselves he suggested they went out to buy more discreet clothes. "You want to look like me, gentlemen. This is my Edinburgh garb. In London a bit of frill perhaps, but Edinburgh folks like both to swank and save together. And good boots." (He shook his head at their dirty brogues.) "You have money I take it?

Iain nodded, Seumas grunted "Lots" while simultaneously, Jamie said "If not, I can always lend you some."

They protested at this offer. "We have all our worldly wealth with us. We intend buying some base for trading in Edinburgh and France. Wines, mostly, we feel. We must pick your brains over dinner. We are already much in your debt. Let's go then and transform ourselves into Sassenachs."

As they were about to set out Jamie's servant Rollo came in. "Perhaps gentlemen....." Jamie began, then stopped. They raised eyebrows in query. "No, never mind, gentlemen. I was going to suggest you could leave Rollo to guard your wealth but you cannot be too careful. One man might not be enough. Keep your bags with you all the time. The Lowlands are wicked, quite wicked."

The brothers, who had briefly tensed, thanked him for his concern. "Don't worry, We take great care. A light burns all night and the bags are tied to one of us and the other lies armed and awake." They did not notice the wry smile on Jamie's face nor the frown on Rollo's not the look that passed between them. They went off on their first step to becoming gentlemen of the Lowlands.

They actually had a hilarious time, entering into the spirit of the transformation, and if Jamie was generous with their money he was as open-handed with his own. He left them before the inn fire and vanished for an hour, returning with two silver-topped sticks. "Very useful for traders, gentlemen. This pattern here is marked in inches and the sticks weigh exactly three pounds. Portable weights and measures'' he laughed (and he was always laughing, teasing, without being in the least condescending.) ''You never know when you might like to make discreet measures of your own. See, on the top of each I have had your initials scribed.'' They looked, and there saw a pattern of holly leaves with sets of initials incorporated. ''Holly is the Macmillan badge, I trust?'' Jamie smiled, pretending to a doubt. They were delighted with this personal touch, and then astonished when he showed them one last trick. Each innocent stick was hollow and contained a long, narrow sword blade. When they had recovered from their excitement Iain (rather soulfully) asked what on earth the sword-sticks would cost them.

''But gentlemen, these are a gift. I have enjoyed your company this day. And truth, I am also slightly tinged with romantic jealousy. Ten years ago I rode an old nag over the Mounth with hardly a penny to my name. You remind me of my good fortune, and my departing youth. Come, let us drink to successful years ahead,'' and, brushing aside their thanks, Jamie swept them through to the dining room. Seumas placed the bags on the floor and placed his feet on top of them. Looking up he caught Rollo watching from the door and a frown flickered across his brow. Jamie had noticed and quickly said ''Don't worry about Rollo. He never lets *me* out of his sight. I'm his money bags.'' They all laughed, then Jamie added more sombrely. ''It is all right for you. There are two of you to sleep together and or stand back to back. Rollo is my insurance. He's no brighter than anyone else from the Howe o' Fife, but, eh, he's a bonnie fighter. And he doesn't blab.''

''Lucky you,'' Seumas said.

''No! The Devil take the luck. It's hard work. Years of it. So, when you can, you enjoy it. I've made it, gentlemen. You are on your way.''

It was a merry evening. The fare seemed better (Rollo had paid the kitchen staff to ensure it was) and the wine was quite definitely better. Iain however drank little, on the grounds of a stomach complaint, but, in truth, it was his night to stay awake. Seumas smiled at him and raised a glass of rubies to his lips. The conversation turned quite casually to their plans and before the evening was out Jamie knew the (surprisingly large) sum they had for investing and was able to make all sorts of suggestions for setting up in Edinburgh. They agreed to stay in his house till they could obtain lodgings. Jamie seemed to know everyone. He described a visit to Achnacarry when Locheil had secretly obtained swords delivered inside the innocent-looking bales of cloth. Jamie was perhaps rather indiscreet in his Jacobite sympathies but the Macmillans would only agree with him. Before they went to bed they all stood and drank a silent toast, holding their glasses out across the finger bowl of water in the centre of the table.,

Two hours later Rollo carefully opened the door of their room A candle still burned but the brothers lay asleep. Seumas snoring heavily and Iain breathing deep and even. Their breeks lay on a chair by the bed. The money bags were a lump under the blanket between them. As Rollo gently closed the door Iain opened one eye and shut it again in a wink that was not a wink. The dirk was still in his hand. Rollo reported to Grant. ''Snoring their heads off. Another night or two and they'll be completely careless.'' Before daybreak Rollo was on his way to Edinburgh, commissioned to furnish a certain house, enrol servants and enquire about the sailings that week from Leith to London. The smile on Jamie's face as he watched his partner depart was not at all a pleasant one.

Over breakfast Jamie put forward some ideas that ''had come to him in the night.'' He, Jamie, was going to London in a few days. Why did they not come with him? He knew of a prime property not far from St. Paul's which would be a good investment. There was dock space just ten minutes away. It would be more expensive than Edinburgh but the returns would be infinitely greater. Half the morning had gone before they finally mounted. Jamie explained that he had sent Rollo on to warn his household of their coming. Three well-mounted gentlemen were unlikely to be molested. Two of them actually never gave it a thought. Dr. Johnston thirty years later only put into words their thoughts that the best road in Scotland was the one leading to London. They may have given silver-tongued Jamie Grant the hundred best reasons for maybe staying in Edinburgh but they had every intention of going to London. So they rode on, between the Pentlands and Corstorphine Hill, and entered the city under the bastions of its castle on the rock.

Jamie's town house lay hard by the Canongate, midway between the Castle and Holyrood Palace. There was a bustle of servants and several lined up to greet their master warmly. The two pretty maids were not slow in presenting their cheeks for a kiss. Jamie Grant obviously lived well. Eating and drinking were just becoming the gargantuan indulgence of the period. Hospitality was still liberal. Two friends of Jamie's had called and were persuaded to stay for dinner. It was strictly a social evening. Business was only touched on in general terms. Their particular plans were not discussed.

Jamie himself insisted on Iain and Seumas placing their money bags on the dresser and sitting where they could see them. "I think I can trust my servants, gentlemen, but you never know these days. Rollo I'd trust with my life, indeed, I owe it to him, but servants are the great eavesdroppers and letter filchers." The brothers gave a bit of a start at the mention of letters but Jamie rambled on with his good-natured chat. He was very kindness itself. They had been wondering how they could guard their bags without giving offence. It was all very well dining at an inn with one's feet on a small fortune but you could hardly do that in a gentleman's house, yet leaving their hard-gathered savings in their room would have been unthinkable. There was no key for the door and it had a window looking over a rather smelly back lane, a "close" as Jamie called it. Their host seemed, uncannily, to read their minds and had this nice ability to put them at their ease. Behind the laughter and the banter they realised there lay an astute brain.

The conviviality of the meal mellowed everyone and the two

Edinburgh guests were soon good companions to the strangers to the city. Jamie told of a trading run to the Netherlands when they'd been set-upon by footpads and Rollo and he literally stood back to back and fended off twice their number of attackers. "It is not all ledgers and banking profits, gentlemen," he laughed. "It is not always wine and linen either, eh, Jamie" one of the guests suggested. Jamie blandly replied, "Any service to one's king is naturally not a matter for accounting. One can hope for a return one day perhaps. Monarchs are not ungrateful to those who help them to a throne." Iain and Seumas were a bit astonished at such openly-expressed opinions but they were obviously those of all present and they had noticed there would be a lull in the conversation, or some intervening irrelevancy, anytime a serving wench was present. Rollo, who served the drink (and partook of some himself) never left the room. For a Lowlander he seemed to be quite a formidable character. Master may have drunk well but the servant did not. Drinking set them a problem. Poor Iain was forced into another evening of abstinence (they could hardly be dyspeptic night and night about!) while Seumas made the most of the good things offered.

The ship to London sailed in two days' time. Jamie hoped that Iain's sleeplessness would tell by then. They wanted no bloodshed pointing to a crime but if Edinburgh did not see their robbery committed, then there was always the ship. The sea could swallow victims and evidence together. Jamie proposed a toast to the good ship *Venture*. After dinner they played cards and Iain and Seumas in the end had won most of the money. Twice Jamie went to a small chest and brought more money, which he then lost. At the end of the night Iain suggested they should pay all the money back. They were not used to gaming with such sums and it would be on their consciences. Jamie laughed off their suggestion. Such sums were normal between gentlemen. Maybe the next night he would win it all back. It was late before the party broke up and the Highlanders were able to gain their room.

They discussed the evening's events in whispers and seemed

contented -- but they nevertheless mounted guard again. "Did you see the silver cups in yon chest?" Iain asked, and Seumas replied, "He is remarkably confident and careless is our Jamie. The papers in that chest could hang him, yet he is unconcerned". "Oh, maybe that is his genius. A careless and casual Whig merchant to the world, obviously prosperous and straight. Who could possibly suspect his motives? Perhaps he would seek to draw us into his Jacobite plots."

Iain walked up and down the room thereafter for he felt if he lay down he would simply fall asleep. "Och, just sleep" Seumas yawned. "We're in the house of a friend. I doubt if anyone could win past that grim guard-dog Rollo." Rollo, his ear to the door, grinned at this comment and went off to report progress to his partner. Jamie Grant seemed well content. "Tomorrow, we'll have them. We can try the wenches."

A suggested excursion the next day was turned down by Iain and Seumas; with just twenty four hours before the *Venture* sailed from Leith they preferred to stay within the security of the house. Jamie concurred readily enough and Rollo was sent off to the port to determine the time they should be aboard. When he came back three hours later it was to report a six o'clock sailing. There were curses all round at the unearthly hour but tides don't ebb and flow with man's convenience in view. They debated whether they should move to a Leith inn for the night or ride from Edinburgh and, at Jamie's kind insistence, decided on the latter course, which seemed the more secure option.

It was a restless sort of day. Nobody seemed able to settle and the evening was largely curtailed with the necessity of an early departure. They played cards for an hour and Jamie and Rollo, who was brought in as a fourth hand, could hardly manage to lose the games -- and money -- as was intended. But they felt bait enough had been laid, and swallowed.

The Macmillans excused themselves on the grounds of being a wee bit tired and went to their room. "Sleep well, both of you" said Jamie as he turned to leave their bedroom. "Aye, I'm sure we will" came Iain's yawned reply. As he descended the stair Jamie expelled a long breath so the candle set the shadows dancing. He muttered: "Aye, the night's the night, surely, surely," and went to plot the final act with his henchman.

At an ungodly hour of the clock they crept to the door of the Highlanders' room. They listened. Silence. Distantly, they heard two toll on the Tron Church clock. Rollo eased the door open. The room lay in semi-darkness, lit only with the wash of a summer moon. As they peered in Jamie's hand tightened on Rollo's arm. The saddle bags lay on a chair while the two lay gently snoring on the bed. Like a wraith Rollo glided over and bore off their booty. Jamie carefully locked the door from the outside. They crept down the stairs. "Clear the house of all the hired furnishings" they ordered the so-called servants. "When you have done meet us at the house at Duddingston and go round by the Red Craigs and the loch. None must go near Leith this day". As the men set about their toil, he commanded to one "You, Patterson, bring me my chest, personally, before the rest."

They led their horses out and rode off round the hill. Once past the guards and the last houses they broke into slightly hysterical laughter. "Oh, Jamie, it was cruel! it was like taking bannocks from a bairn!" Jamie slapped a hand on the heavy bags by his knees. "Deed, aye, Alex, and are we no a bonny pair?" They rode singing , round under the pillared rocks of the Red Craig. Jamie turned to Alex Rollo. "Next week, I think we could do with a celebration. Shall we ride post to London? Besides, I've a letter in yon chest which is addressed to his Lordship Grange." Rollo sat silent a moment, and his reply was whispered. "A lesser pair of rogues might have had scruples at robbing fellow Jacobites." Then he laughed, "The chicken tastes the same whatever the hue of its feathers. London! Aye, let's to London." Passing the loch on the mossy road Jamie threw the key of the Macmillans' sleeping quarters outwards into the darkness. There was a splash, and the ripples ringed outwards in the gloaming. They rode, chortling, in to the village, passing as they did the house where a year later Charles Edward Stuart was to lodge. A heron flapped a solitary flight over the valley and a gowk mocked from up on the hill.

At the same time as the key of the locked room sank into Duddingston Loch two gentlemen with ornate sticks, a small chest and little other baggage boarded the brig *Venture*. She was standing off for the May Island before Grant and Rollo (which were not their names) discovered their duplicity had been trumped. Iain and Seumas Macmillan were not real names either. They stood by the rail in the grey light of early dawn reading a letter they had taken from the chest from the house in Edinburgh. "We will be well paid in London for this night's work, brother Iain", the reader commented. The other smiled, "We have been well enough paid already. Several night's good lodging, good company, good food, good wine. Even money thrown at us, and silver goblets and fine sword-sticks. They were unbelievable. Unbelievable. Of all people they had to pick they chose us. Oh, it's cruel. It was like taking carraway cake from a child. But it shows the despicable nature of these Jacobites. They would even rob each other."

The mate of the *Venture* called to 'Seumas' and 'Iain' from the after-hatch. "Mr. Campbell, Mr. Fraser, would you like to step down for some breakfast?" They did so, and over the bread the cheese and ale they lapsed into further periods of mirth.

"A penny for your thoughts?"

"I was just picturing the faces of those two tricksters when they open the saddlebags with our 'treasure'."

It was a scene worth picturing. The saddlebags had contained several horse shoes, a broken blade and several other bits and pieces of scrap metal.

THE POOR DOG'S TAIL

A collie raced the car up the drive and two cairn terriers brought a ball for us to throw as we walked up to the porch. The place bounced with dogs. "It always does," sighed mother. Odd people wheezed about, conversing in doggie language. In other words, the stage was set before we arrived. I do not hold myself responsible for what happened.

Mother had often described the place. "A rambling old farmhouse above the bay and looking across to the Cuillin. Wonderful cooking, of course, and such nice local girls. Corramonachan really is heavenly."

So it was not too difficult to drag her away from a home that itself resembled a guest house with its constant stream of friends and relatives, and, with father, take a ten-day trip to the far north-west. I was just back from the second polar balloon flight, so was only too glad of a break from press and radio demands. Father has bad eyesight so no longer drives. I could look forward to driving over some of the remotest roads in Britain.

We were pursued by rain up to Ross and Sutherland but when we crossed to Skye on the way south again the grey, sad weather gave way to a watery sunshine that left the Black Cuillin glittering and bright.

Corramonachan *was* heavenly.

It lay in complete seclusion at the end of a long shingly drive off the hill road which in turn parted from the main Armadale road halfway down the peninsula. The new shoots of bracken were still in tight curls and the wild hyacinths were a blue blaze along the banks of alder and hazel. The burns ran, creamy and noisy, to the foamy

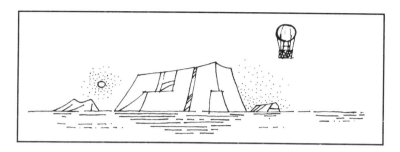

edge of the sea. The landscape quivered with the expectancy that follows rain.

The guest house was crowded. Old Mrs. Macmillan was very apologetic that I would have to make do with a fold-down couch in the small dining-room. "Really dreadful! After all, your mother and father are old friends of Corramonachan."

After my recent three months of roughing it, *any* bed was comfort. I said so.

"Of course, Mr. Martin, I've read all about your trips. How very exciting! Really, I'm awfully sorry. I'd no idea, Mrs. Martin, that the famous Fraser Martin was your son. You never said. What will everybody say?...."

I slipped out and joined father in the sun room overlooking the moving silver of the sea. Clouds were streaming off Blaven.

In the corner a guest was reading *The Times*. He gave a baleful, military glare over its defensive pages. Puffy, red cheeks flanked a red nose and the stained moustache hung down lamely. At his feet lay a naked-looking bull terrier. I could swear it drank, too. Its watery eye never left father and me. We found ourselves talking in whispers.

Dinner was delicious -- and dogs were excluded. We were made a foursome by the addition of a middle-aged Glaswegian in a kilt. "Ah'm the outdoor breed," he explained. He had an enormous girth round which the poor kilt was strained out of shape. He kept popping open his sporran to produce a large, red handkerchief with which he mopped his brow. "It's close weather. Ah cannae staun it. Neither can Jock, ma wee pal."

For the rest of the meal, we heard of Jock, the most wonderful Scottie in the world, pal of many a ramble from Balloch or Aberfoyle. "He'll be lying at the fit o ma bed the noo, the wee sowl." Luckily Mrs. Macmillan was out of earshot. She has categorical beliefs about dogs and beds.

At the next table sat a distracting brunette. She talked not at all so I assumed she could not be a dog owner. Perhaps she would be good company later in the evening. She wore a caramel-coloured knitted outfit and gazed unsmilingly at the babble of guests. Our eyes met. She raised one eyebrow meaningfully.

I half giggled -- only to be brought to heel.

"It wasnae funny, Mr. Martin. He might hae been run ower."

After dinner I escaped the dog house and walked along the cliffs. The old collie came along too, then a panting made me stop while a scruffy and utterly charming Yorkshire terrier caught up. His shaggy coat was full of burrs, and matted and muddy. There was blood on his nose and his eyes glittered with fun.

"Hello, Mischief!" I greeted him for I had heard from father about this character. He lived at Corramonachan (as did the old collie) and had often walked with father on previous visits.

"He's a little devil and runs wild about the place."

He covered three times the ground I did. There was excitement in every bush and quarry down every hole. For ten minutes he was away over the grey rocks after a hare, his yapping coming faintly on the breeze. I arrived back with wet shoes and a 'filthy wee dug' -- according to our Glasgow friend who was exercising his Jock on a tartan lead round the garden.

The house dogs padded off kitchenwards leaving a trail of paw-prints and I squelched upstairs. Later I walked into the lounge to find father was showing photographs of my recent expedition to an over-dressed, ample-bosomed woman. Large amber beads, mauve cardigan, lovat tweeds. I shuddered and took her fat, spongy hand.

"Look at this, Reginald dear. Isn't it marvellous?"

"Yes, mother."

Reginald was perched on the edge of his chair, looking unenthusiastically -- and upside down -- at the prints. He reminded me instantly of a Pekingese, a snuffly 'yes-mother-no-mother' pet.

"What deep purpose drives you to such desperate adventures in distracting places, Mr. Martin?" he asked wheezily.

I gave the scripted reply that evaded the question (it has no answer) and looked round for escape from this latest trap. I was on holiday, after all.

"Do fetch Ping and Pong, Reginald dear. I'm sure Mr. Martin would love to meet them. So like huskies in some ways."

I winced.

"Yes, mother."

It was like a ghastly cartoon come to life. Scotty sat in a corner mumbling away to Jock, ex-Indian army had commandeered the other corner and with his bull terrier established a defensive position, the collie lay before the fire in aged serenity, mother had the armchair and father was showing the photographs on the couch. Reginald could only be going to fetch a pair of Pekingese. How could animals so suit their owners?

The next moments were hectic.

The door beside Scotty opened and the lanky girl came in with a tray.

"Supper-time, folks," she called.

At the same time Reginald entered the other door with the inevitable pekes. Then the Yorkshire terrier appeared (I don't know where from) and made a growling rush for the new arrivals.

I lunged out to grab him and somehow stood on his tail. Mischief naturally screamed, the pekes tore loose and one immediately dived through the legs of the supper-bearer. Her tray went flying, the milk jug scored on Reginald's mother, the sugar on father and the crockery over most of the carpet. The collie and bull terrier dived for the biscuits and Mischief, looking for revenge, bit the nearest leg, which happened to be the colonel's. He let fly with his cane, missed the dog, but caught the bending brunette, who landed on top of the pekes.

Things became confused.

But I forget much else. My dive having missed. I found myself gripping an ankle above a heavy brogue shoe. I gazed up into a furious countenance, dripping milk and throwing milky pictures of balloons about while shouting hysterically. I leaped up, cracked my head on the mantelpiece, which toppled a marble statue from its pedestal. Two cracks were enough for my skull, and I lapsed into happy unconsciousness -- luckily on top of my mother.

The doctor, the vet, the local constable, several maids and both Mr. and Mrs. Macmillan were needed to patch and repair flesh and nerves that night. My parents appeared at breakfast and were served by a girl who sniggered the whole time.

Mrs. Macmillan was very nice about it all. I was not allowed up before eleven. I still had a buzzing head as I drove off with my parents before lunch. Mischief and the old collie raced down the long drive behind us. The Cuillin lay turquoise on the horizon and a red sail splashed its way beyond the headland. We turned to the hill road and the dogs stood smiling after us.

I had a telegram today from the brunette. It comes from Grindewald, and reads:

'Good wishes for expedition, Fraser darling. See you at Corramonachan on return. Remember the poor dog's tail.'

I could not make out if the last bit was a query or an order. No matter. This dog got caught. I've promised her it will be the last expedition.

JEAN LOUIS AND THE PAINTED LADIES

Jean Louis was called in because he was an *'alpiniste'* and knew the High Atlas ranges well. The British Council in Rabat had received what seemed an odd request from the University of Bristol: could they help with organising a spring expedition to some of the high passes in the Atlas where they wanted to capture and mark migrating butterflies with the intriguing name of 'Painted Ladies'.

The mind boggled somewhat at the thought of pursuing Painted Ladies over the hills. "Imagine asking the local Caïd about *that,*" old Partridge commented over a *café au lait* on the terrace of the Balima. "*Pas de problem*" Ivor Rushton grinned. "There's no need to go through all the channels. Climbers wander up into the Atlas all the time. There's porters and huts and everything. Bit run down perhaps, but the CAF are still active."

"CAF. What's that?"

"*Club Alpin Français.* I'm actually a member and hope to get up there myself. I've maps and the old Dreish and Lépiney Guide."

"Well, it looks as if you can head for the hills officially on this one."

"Sorry, in the spring I'm stuck with the weekly language classes, but a friend of mine, Jean Louis Froment, I know would be free. He knows the Atlas already as he grew up in Marrakech. Just graduated, in France, but in no hurry to settle into a job. He'd lap it up. Speaks good English...."

Which is how Jean Louis came to make contact with Painted Ladies. The English students tended to refer to them quite unfeelingly by their Latin name *Vanessa cardui* and they also had an interest in Bath Whites or *Pontia daplidice.* Maybe it was the very name 'Painted Ladies' that so caught the fancy of Jean Louis. He was an imaginative, lively young Frenchman, after all.

"Ivor, I will go anywhere, anytime, there are ladies involved, painted or not" he had teased Rushton on having the subject broached.

Jean Louis was thorough, too, and even before the Bristol department contacted him direct he began to read up what he could find about these butterflies. It was fascinating. It was so fascinating that Jean Louis could hardly contain himself for the two months before he'd be heading south from Marrakech over the Haouz Plains to the gleaming snows that rim the horizon south of that bustling city. One Sunday afternoon he and Rushton sat in the Moorish Cafe overlooking the Bou Regreg and the town of Salé opposite. From Salé came the term 'Sally Rover', some of those pirates being of English origins. One had built some of the Kasbah defences where they sat.

"Ivor, do you realise these beautiful, delicate, flying angels come all the way across the Sahara from West Africa? They cross that blasted waste in tens of thousands only to run up against the Atlas Mountains. Djebel Toubkal is 3,165 metres -- that's about 13,500 feet in your funny measurements -- the highest point in all North Africa. They then cross or go round this colossal barrier, pass the Straits to Spain and then continue over the notorious Bay of Biscay to end up in the south west of England. *C'est formidable!*"

In his excitement he sent his glass of *thé à la menthe* on to the tiles.

Ivor laughed. "Stop flying, Jean Louis. You're not a butterfly yet," then added "Look, there's a butterfly. Is it a Painted Lady?"

A butterfly had landed on the soggy lumps of sugar from Jean Louis's tea and stayed, sipping greedily, till a blundering bee, after the same free nectar, blundered into it and the butterfly flapped away over the bougainvillea towards Salé.

Jean Louis had shaken his head and went on to describe just what a Painted Lady looked like.

"Good God" Ivor commented, "You've still never seen one and yet you're quite infatuated!"

"Oh, yes, quite infatuated," Jean Louis agreed. "I dream about them every night. Much safer than the painted ladies of the Rue de Masa in the Medina."

He was only half joking.

Jean Louis called in officially before setting off to meet the Bristol students at the Hotel du Foucauld in Marrakech. He seemed to have everything well organised: a bus laid on to Asni, where, after a night at the Hotel du Toubkal, they would proceed, on mules, up the River Mizane to Arround, where there was a CAF *refuge* which would be their base. Several higher *refuges* at about the 3,000 metre mark would be visited in turn and above them were the snowy cols, with heights of up to 3,800 metres, which would be places, they hoped, for ambushing the migrant *papillons*. Both Partridge and Rushton had to listen to the life cycle of *Vanessa cardui* being enthusiastically described. Later, Partridge commented "Seems an efficient enough lad, for a Frenchman, but a bit crazy, if you ask me. All he has to do is look after our chaps and see they don't upset the locals and yet he seems to have gone overboard about *his* Painted Ladies. He doesn't own them!"

"It is fascinating, though," Ivor commented. "They make that journey, year after year, from West Africa to the West Country. None ever go back -- so how on earth do they know where they're going? I thought bird migration was quite something. This is even more astonishing."

"I'm sure it is," old Partridge smiled indulgently. "Monsieur Froment seems to have infected you with his enthusiasm." He paused. "I'm sorry you're stuck here. I think you'd have taken leave to go with your butterfly friend. Instead of which we'd better get stuck into the monthly returns."

Jean Louis and the English students took to each other at once. There were six of them, rather self-conscious entomologists, to whom rushing about on the mountains with big butterfly nets had seemed a bit ridiculous 'in front of a Frog', but Jean Louis had turned out to be as enthusiastic as they really were, and as knowledgeable. The rushing about was pretty spasmodic anyway.

They would cross a side pass into one of the next valleys to gain a hut, like the *Refuge Lépiney* at 3,050 metres, then, next day, spend three hours with ice axes and crampons slogging to the *tizi* (pass) to sit there all day with never a butterfly putting in an appearance. A few days of that could pall, but Jean Louis simply led them up the nearer peaks while they waited. Though none of them were climbers they ascended quite a few of the easier major summits. It was all good fun. Whenever they retreated to Arround, Jean Louis would natter to the locals in their guttural speech and an hour after dark they'd go off for a *tagine* or a *cous cous* in some local house. Jean Louis made friends everywhere in no time.

"But I have not met my love, the Painted Ladies" he complained one night as they sat replete, sipping glasses of scalding *thé à la menthe*, the national drink of Morocco.

"About time we did," the leader said. "It would be embarrassing to go back empty handed."

"We'll not exactly do that. We've specimens, enough."

And so they had. God knows how many butterflies perish in the desert or over the sea, but the snows of the Atlas were spotted in places by hundreds of dead Painted ladies, many of them lying at the foot of inch-deep hollows.

"The heat of the sun on their corpses sinks them into the snow like that," someone told Jean Louis.

Jean Louis dreamed every night about his Painted Ladies. In his dream he would rush about with his large net, dancing over the mountain tops and whooping with joy as he scooped with the huge white muslin bag. He was the greatest Painted Lady hunter of all time -- even if he'd never set eyes on a living specimen.

They were sitting on the Tizi n'Tamatert, one of the side passes, returning from three fruitless days at Tachddirt, when Jean Louis noticed a butterfly dancing past. It looked like a Painted Lady.

He chewed his hard bread and salami silently, watching. A few minutes later there was another, then another. "*Regardez!* "he yelled, spluttering out his lunch. In a few minutes the numbers built up: irregular individuals became dancing scores which became blowing hundreds until the pass was a whole gale of winged movement. It was like being in a Quantock beechwood in an autumn storm. They all went Painted Lady crazy.

"What's the code?" Jean Louis yelled.

"We'll use yesterday's: one yellow dot."

Frantically they dug out tubes of paint, fitted their nets together, and went into action. What the local Berber shepherd boy (aged about seven) made of the spectacle has not been recorded. In his eyes seven crazy *Nazarenes* went charging about waving huge white flags on the end of poles and periodically whammed them to the ground where they knelt with bottoms in the air in some mysterious rite that had nothing to do with facing Mecca.

They were actually, direct from the Reeves tubes, marking the thorax of each butterfly with a spot of yellow paint, then letting them go again. In two hours they 'spotted' 3,276 Painted Ladies. (Such was this enthusiasm that one of the students actually caught a Painted Lady which bore a yellow spot!) Jean Louis was not the only one who shouted out in excited dreaming that night. They all agreed it had been one of the most astonishing experiences any of them had ever had.

For the record, six of those marked butterflies were caught again in the West Country and two more were caught in Clifton itself. One of the party wrote at once to Jean Louis, mentioning the awe he felt on handling one of these delicate creatures with the single yellow mark on it. "I thought back to the Tizi n'Tamatert and that amazing migration. And this tiny thing, with what mind-blowing navigational mechanism, is now here (an exciting enough journey for us). But for a butterfly! '*Formidable* !' as you always kept saying. Scientists are often called unimaginative but in the face of such wonders all we can do is marvel. Even the old professor got quite excited. It will be long enough before we gather all the information. We'll send you the eventual paper. Remember our motto: Up the Painted Ladies!''

Jean Louis did not read the card for long enough, for his connection with Painted Ladies was to take him to unimagined countries of the mind and it was a long time before he came down to earth again.

But to revert to the Bristol gang in the Atlas. After that first successful day their two weeks of waiting was soon forgotten. They were run off their feet chasing and 'spotting' the butterflies. From seven sites they marked 22,000 Painted Ladies (and 3,000 Bath Whites) of which about 148 were recovered in England. The statistical analysis and all the other studies need not concern us. It was a highly successful expedition. There was just one disappointment.

They had planned to spend up to two weeks camping at two places on the coast, Mogador and Oulidia, to see if there was a separate migration round, as well as over, the Atlas. Their earlier lack of success meant that this part of the study had to be abandoned and they doubted if it would be followed up, for the regular British reason -- the department was skint.

Jean Louis at once cried that this was not good enough. He would go, forthwith, to Oulidia (it would be too late for Mogador, further south) and carry on the programme. ''I am, what you say 'hooked' on these little beauties. I live butterflies. I dream butterflies. I will watch for the Painted Ladies.''

After an outrageously enjoyable traditional Moroccan dinner in the richly-decorated Foucauld, he saw the party off on their Marrakech-Casa.-London flight, still talking nineteen-to-the dozen and shouting ''Up the Painted Ladies'' across the barriers, to the bewilderment of more staid British tourists.

Jean Louis then sped to Oualidia and set up camp by the shore: a mix of jagged reefs and miles of sand backed by salt lagoons, much favoured by godwit, stilt and flamingo. Blind to the ornithological richness he paced the days through on his dedicated entomological search. No flutter of a butterfly wing escaped his eye, and every night, all night, he dreamed of Painted Ladies.

On the third night he scared the wits out of the two local boys he'd employed to guard camp and cook for him. They heard him "roaring like a lion" and when they peered out of their tent they saw a near-naked figure rushing around with a great, white, round banner crying a phrase over and over again. In a few days they would imitate Jean Louis's cry of 'Painted Ladies, Painted Ladies' and snigger together over the stove.

Lying on his camp bed Jean Louis would gaze up into the white dome of his mosquito net and imagine *he* was the Painted Lady and the mosquito net was the butterfly net about to descend on him. His dreams became nightmares as the days passed and there were still no Painted Ladies. He was probably not helped by accepting the *kif* pipe his camp followers produced after supper each night. He roamed the dunes for miles each day, walking which became more and more frenzied. He never left the butterfly net behind, nor a tube of the Reeve's vermilion which would be the first colour code he'd use on *his* Painted Ladies. It took about two weeks for enthusiasms to become obsession. His frightened boys then vanished, taking half the camp equipment with them. Jean Louis hardly noticed. He barely ate. Life crystallised (or should we say chrysalised?) to the *idée fixe* of a huge butterfly, a magic painted Lady. "*C'est moi, un papillon merveilleux.*"

Jean Louis couldn't have told you how or when the transformation took place. He dreamed of Painted Ladies, then he knew *he* was a Painted Lady dreaming he was Jean Louis. There must have been some chrysalis stage to this metamorphosis. He didn't notice how he emerged from the cocoon of the past to become a Painted Lady migrating up the coast, but *that* was the reality.

When his parents hadn't heard from him for a month, after he'd phoned from the Foucauld in Marrakech, they got in touch with the British Council. They had heard no more than his father: Jean

Louis had gone off to Oualidia to look for Painted Ladies. Ivor felt duty bound to go with Froment *père* to Oualidia. They found an abandoned camp, and, with the help of the *gendarmerie* two very frightened youths reluctantly told their story. Police threats simply silenced them, but Ivor found a regular application of francs worked wonders. Not that the story that emerged made any sense. Jean Louis appeared to have had a dose of *cafard*, to have gone bonkers. But Ivor could hardly say that to Jean Louis's old man. He didn't need to in the end. The old man suggested as much to him.

They returned to Rabat and life resumed its normal routine of teaching and good works. Ivor had a couple of letters from the Bristol students, one a formal sort of 'Thank You', the other of a more personal nature following his letter explaining Jean Louis's disappearance. There the matter rested.

But as Allah brings the sun and the rain, and the rivers flow to the sea, so this business was not yet over. Ivor was sitting in the Moorish cafe one Sunday afternoon two months later. He was reading a novel while enjoying the usual *thé à la menthe*, with a *corne de gazelle*, when a cheery voice hailed him. "Hello, Ivor, old cock. 'Up the Painted Ladies', as we used to say."

He just about fell off the bench. It was Jean Louis, Jean Louis as thin as a ghost, dressed in a malodorous and tatty *djellaba* and sandals with car tyre soles: a real tramp.

"Could I have a *thé* please?" he asked.

They sat drinking. Ivor was consumed with curiosity but before he could bring himself to ask any questions Jean Louis said "No questions, old chap. *Après, peut-être*. Much more important, can you kit me out like a Christian again? And give me a bath? I'm not going home like this and I haven't a *sou* for anything."

Naturally Ivor complied.

Jean Louis reappeared in Rabat society just as if he had never been absent for something like five months. He took a job with *Le Matin* and was as good company as ever. All he could tell Ivor, however, was that he woke one night in the tent at Oualidia with the horrors on him and convinced his mosquito net was coming down on him just like a net on a poor butterfly. The next thing he remembered was a fisherman's hut near Magazan whose simple occupants had apparently taken pity on one of Allah's sons and clothed and fed and nursed him for God knows how long.

"I walked into Magazan but nobody French would listen to me. On the *plage* my appearance so scared one family that they fled.

Madame dropped her purse and I ran after her but they fluttered up to a gendarme in hysterics so I thought it better to vanish down into the *souks.* The purse had just enough for buses back to Rabat and I didn't really have any misgivings about using it."

"Jean Louis made it all sound like a bit of a lark" Ivor reported back to Partridge. "God know what hell he's been through."

Two of the team from Bristol managed to scrape together enough money to come out next Easter vac. and Ivor and Jean Louis joined them for a climbing holiday in the Atlas. They climbed Jebel Toubkal, highest of all, and had a great time together. They saw one big migration of Painted Ladies, but it was Ivor who was most excited about that. "Old hat to us, you know" Jean Louis joked.

They went directly from Marrakech to Mogador (now Essaouira, as Magazan is now El Jadida) for a week of relaxing on the sands, pigging in the seafood restaurants and just enjoying the unique flavour of this forgotten walled city of the sea winds. Jean Louis insisted they took a day to visit Oualidia. The others had reservations about his returning there, but the visit was a success. Jean Louis was the life and soul of the holiday from start to finish, and there were no inhibitions about discussing Painted Ladies.

On their first night at Mogador they found Jean Louis up an alley near the *Mellah,* fingering a roll of muslin in one of the *souks* given over to cloth of all kinds. He looked a bit sheepish.

"Well, you never know, do you? If the Painted Ladies start coming up the coast while we're here we couldn't just do *nothing.* So I've found all the necessary to make nets, and dye's no problem.

What is it your Boy Scouts say, eh, 'Be prepared?' I'm prepared!''

He led them, laughing, back to the Place Moulay el Hassan for a last *café* under the feathery Norfolk Island palms.

Ivor and Jean Louis saw the English lads through the check-in at the airport then raced up to the balcony to watch them walk out to their plane. The English two turned on the top of the steps and yelled over to them: ''Up the Painted Ladies!''

In unison Ivor and Jean Louis yelled back the same catch phrase: ''Up the Painted Ladies!''

That night it was Ivor who could not sleep well for thinking about Jean Louis and the Painted Ladies. As for Jean Louis he had gone down to the Rue de Masa and -- eventually - slept very well with one of its painted ladies.

THE ORNITHOLOGISTS

Wee Davie Sproul and Jock Tamson lay on the grass beside the tent with the deep contentment of youth. They had hardly said a word that morning. It would have been a kind of sacrilege if they had done so.

They had woken at four to the silvery, secretive, first light of spring. It was the dawn chorus that woke them. They lay thrilled while bird after bird joined in: blackbirds, a missel thrush, a robin; these they could pick out, but there were so many others still unknown. Neither spoke. The tickly blankets kept off the raw edge of dawn and the aches of the day before had gone during the night.

They were ordinary boys but no less interesting for that. Over the winter a new teacher had come to the school and inspired in many of the boys an interest in bird-watching. They were 'Ornithologists' in fact -- not young nest-robbers or those who used gutties on the speugs. They were proud of the big word and what it meant for them. They were proud of being Paisley boys, too, (better than Glasgow any day) and they were proud of their bikes, earned by delivering rolls all through the bitter winter. Their fathers had given them a bird book and a pair of binoculars (second-hand from the Barras) as reward for their hard saving.

Their joy was complete when allowed to plan a camping trip to the Trossachs. The B.B. had lent them the small tent, and Friday seemed to take years to come. They had hardly heard their mother's "Mine an no get yir shoen wet!" as they pedalled off. The Duke's Pass had almost puggled them and they were glad to lift their bikes over the dyke and put up the tent among the trees near the road skirting Loch Achray. Tea and jammy pieces and they were soon asleep.

Saturday morning soon passed. The weather was balmy as it had been all week. They woke up at six o'clock, had breakfast and then a swim and then another breakfast. This all took time because they kept seeing new birds. A snipe shot its wild way across their clearing, leaving them scrambling for their glasses -- far too late as the bird had gone. A sandpiper took off, too, by the burn; that one took a bit of finding in the book.

A bullfinch had really thrilled them. And all through the morning there was the cuckoo's call, an incessant, echoing mystery. Nobody ever seemed to have SEEN a cuckoo. That was their plan for the afternoon.

They left the burnt frying pan in the burn in disgust (Davie's mother had something to say about that!) and walked along to the hotel. It was full of posh cars and people coming out from lunch. The road was crowded with cars as they turned back.

At once they saw a path rising up into the trees. They looked at each other.

'Cuckoo' came the call from the hills.

Ten minutes later and some hundreds of feet higher they collapsed by the path.

"Whit a pech!" gasped wee Davie.

"Dinna move,"whispered Jock. "There's a bluetit ahint yir lug."

"Well, hoo can ah see it then?" hissed back Davie.

The tit flew to the next tree and they watched it dangle upside down on the end of the swaying birch branch.

'Cuckoo' came the call from higher up the brae.

'Cuckoo' came a call again at no distance at all.

"Come on," they whispered and scrambled off. The tit flitted to the next branch.

The boys inched forward, carefully placing feet between twigs and scarce daring to breathe.

'Cuckoo,' came the distant call.

'Cuckoo,' came the nearer answer.

"Jist roon they rocks!"

They crept round and then stopped dead.

Two blazing eyes glowered at them.

The face surrounding those eyes seemed all hair -- great black locks and matted growth of beard. The man held his hands cupped in front of his thick lips.

The boys stood awkwardly. Wee Davie's lugs had a tinge of red about them.

"Well," said the stranger. It was neither question nor statement.

"We wis tryin tae see a cuckoo," explained Jock uncertainly.

The man lowered his hands quickly and he in turn flushed red.

"It wis you that wis ca'in cuckoo!" blurted out Davie.

There was an awkward silence again.

"Are you interested in birds?" asked the man.

"Aye" they replied together.

"Are you sure?"

"Aye. Sure we're sure."

"You don't steal eggs?" he demanded, and the fierce light danced in his eyes again.

"Jings, naw. We're ornithologists. We ken better."

There was another silence as they stood before those piercing eyes; youth on one side, man on the other, and a great gulf between.

"Would you like to see a cuckoo?"

The gulf contracted to a span.

"Could ye show us yin? Are ye a bird man? Dae ye ken a nest?" the questions poured out.

"Aye," he said softly, and smiled.

Being boys they did not notice the weirdness of the man: his wild face and agitated hands, his dirty clothes and boots. The span had gone. They were all ornithologists. They could trust each other.

They told him of their camp and all they had done and seen. He apparently had seen their camp and watched them eating. This rather upset them as they had tried to be well hidden in case anybody should see them and tell they couldn't camp there. But this man missed nothing.

"Do you see that ant?"

"Aye, sur."

"Well, it's drunk."

"Whit!"

"How dae ye mean?"

"It attacked a caterpillar a a few minutes ago. The caterpillar rolled up tight and oozed out little drops of liquid which the ant licked up as it walked over it. Then it began to stagger and fell over. The caterpillar then went off. I lost sight of it when I started answering the cuckoo."

The boys gasped in amazement.

'Cuckoo,' came the call.

They moved into cover.

"Cuckoo," called out the bearded naturalist.

Davie spotted a movement first. A bird flew down from a tree. He got his glasses to it. "Sparrowhawk maybe?" he suggested.

The man had his eye to a small telescope he had pulled out from some inner pocket. He gave it to Jock.

"What do you say?"

"It's no a hawk. It's no -- is it -- a cuckoo?"

"Yes"

They sucked in their breath. It flew up again and then glided down to a tree stump twenty yards away.

'Cuckoo!'

"Wait till we tell teacher!"

All afternoon the knowledgeable stranger led them about the woods above Loch Achray. They wended towards Ben A'n but the crags were full of noisy climbers so they turned and went down into Glen Finglas.

Their list of new birds grew: mallard, tree-creeper, peewit, woodpecker, a real sparrowhawk (which flashed past and snatched a pipit in front of their very faces), curlew, black-headed gull, dunnock, dipper, chaffinch, heron, willow-warbler -- these were some. On the moor they found seven larks' nests -- at least HE did -- for they could never find them even when they saw the bird fly up.

"That is why," he explained. "They always move several yards away before flying up."

They cut back over the hill in the cool of the evening to avoid the busy road. They were slightly dizzy with the joy of it all.

The strange man left them before they came back to the top of the path. They had shared their pieces, but he would go no further with them.

"I watch here," he said, and somehow his words left a momentary and unreasonable fear. He shook their hands in his massive grip and wished them well. He also gave them a list of all the birds they had seen -- put, as he informed them, in the Wetmore order of classification.

The boys took the steep downward path, chatting merrily and already planning further ornithological expeditions 'doon the watter', and up to the whaup-loud moors near Eaglesham. ("Wi a name like yon!"). They were slightly startled to meet a small party toiling up the path. The first two figures were plainly policemen.

"It wisnae me, officer, honest!" grinned wee Davie.

"Hello, lads!" greeted the placid officer in return -- between puffs while the party collected at his back on the narrow track -- "You haven't seen a man who looks a bit like a tramp anywhere in the wood, now have you?"

"The bird man?" queried Davie.

"Aye, that'll be him, right enough," said a voice behind the constable.

"He hasnae done onything, has he?" Jock asked apprehensively.

"Na, na," said the invisible speaker, pushing forward to explain. "He's a patient at Ballochmore and has some queer-like notions. He's aye trying to get oot bird-watching an such like."

The boys helped as they could and carried on down to the road and their bikes and the long run home.

It was halfway up the Duke's Pass when Davie stopped shoving his heavy cycle and turned to Jock.

"Hey, Jock, dae ye min whit yon doctor-chappie said?"

"When?"

"Aboot the auld man. 'Queer-like notions', he said. 'Like bird-watching.' whit a cheek!"

"Aye, it is that."

"Whit de they ken aboot birds onyway?"

And with a deal of standing on their pedals, they went on up the road for Aberfoyle and distant Paisley.

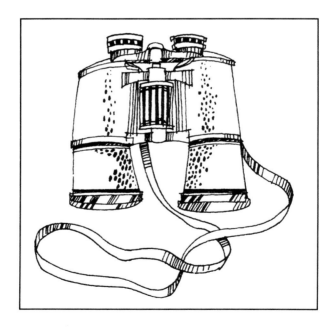

A WHITE BLACKBIRD

Secret Wood was the name used by generations of children. Gus and Will regarded it peculiarly as theirs, for it lay just two magical minutes away from home -- two minutes away as long as the burn was not in spate.

They left their house, 'Dowan Lodge', walked along the pavement a hundred yards to the village boundary where a plain, utilitarian bridge spanned the Hillfoots Burn. Two walls, with a dark green background of trees, was all the fleeting motorist saw; no sign of the span that led to endless adventures. Beyond the bridge, on the left, lay some ruins through which the boys would climb by a window gap, then cross the internal mess of bricks and nettles, and exit out the rear door to tumble down to the burn. This was usually a back garden, garbage-strewn trickle, full of minnows and man-rejected treasure trove: old wheels, picture frames, wire, even water-logged books and furniture. Much of it ended in their tree-house.

The burn led under the road. The cracks in the arched masonry were fringed with pretentious stalactites. It was a private superstition never to break one.

You had to hop from stone to stone, slimy and occasionally treacherous. They had once dragged the big fat biology teacher along to Secret Wood to see a pheasant's nest, but he had been quite hopeless, putting both feet in and simply splashing through. He never came again. Only the village half-wit, Peem, ageless and harmless, seemed able to scramble through no bother. But then, there was nowhere Peem could not go. And there was nothing Peem did not know. None of the teachers knew anything as much as he did about

finding nests, for instance. Gus and Will regarded him as something of a wizard. Adults just bought golf balls off him. They said if ten balls were lost in a day, Peem could always find a dozen.

As you popped out from the bridge, it was like landing in a different world. Secret Wood felt as remote as the Ruwenzori. It was a wee glen, a dell as some of the incomers would say, its banks a tangle of huge, soft butterburr leaves almost roofed over by the fretwork of fir tree branches, elderberry bushes and great beeches. A muddy pool at the south end enabled the boys to provide endless jars of tadpoles for classmates. Raspberries and brambles were guzzled in season. The wood's real defences were simple, though. Never more than a hundred yards wide in all its half mile length, it was hemmed in on both east and west by large fields of barley or corn. The drop from the bridge was not to be contemplated, while the burn ran out through marigold, orchis and cuckoo-spit marshes into the village sewage fields. It was a sanctuary for bird and beast.

The boys had built a big tree-house, for there were endless planks from the house they clambered through to reach the burn entrance, and dead wood enough littered the ground in the wood. An old iron bed (with brass balls at the corners) made the foundation. They thatched it with butterburr leaves and when these shrivelled added old corrugated iron sheeting. It was weatherproof and even had a fire, the height of tree-housemanship! They hoarded sweets in old jelly-jars. The twins could hide away for hours swapping coins from the vast childhood bank of widening experience. Or sulk from parental discipline. Or just be. There was something about the wood that was warm and protective.

The wildlife was completely tame. Rabbits had re-established themselves, and were as likely to sit and watch as scamper off at their coming. The rooks were a pest, though; as soon as you came out from the bridge's dark shadow there would be a loud squawk from the north-end sentry and in seconds the whole tribal hullabaloo informed the wood that the enemy was in the camp.

But even the rooks grudgingly accepted them. The caws soon

died down as word was cawed from tree to tree: it's only Gus and Will White: permitted people.

So they explored every nook and cranny; knew where to find the first snowdrops to take back to mother, or the silken pussy willows, or, at the back end, elderberries for wine or brambles for jelly or flaming branches of beech leaves for the big Chinese vase on the stair.

Occasionally they met Peem there. He was a wizard, of course, for, even though they knew Secret Wood well, in one day he showed them the undiscovered nests of a wagtail, a wren, a moorhen (at the southern edge) and a pheasant (by the eastern cornfield boundary). They had found a robin's, and a coal tit's and there was the obvious rookery, several cushies, and, nearest to their tree-house, a black's. Some they watched year after year. They never took eggs.

Peem was allowed into their tree-house. They were even happy to share their goodies and treasures with him. No other adult would have been admitted; but, as he shared his knowledge, it was a fair enough exchange.

The blackbirds' nest was right next to their tree-house so it naturally came in for regular observation. They had the patience of youth (with its untrammelled hours), so were often content to sit watching for hours on end as the nest was built and occupied.

At first the parent birds, black or brown, would go chacking off in clattering alarm at their approach, but they soon observed a truce. Crumbs, brought along for each visit, acted as 'a diplomatic encouragement', as Will put it. Peem muttered something about 'bribery', but it worked anyway and the mother bird would sit just fifteen feet away, equally happy with periods of mute ornithological enthusiasm or the raucous wrestling and yelling of brotherly ructions.

The male bird was their favourite. The two boys would linger in the evening while the sun silver-beamed among the sturdy trunks and the canopy overhead glittered like a painted chapel ceiling at Evensong. Old blackie would then mount to his stand, cock his shiny eye, and sing. Years later Gus was to say it was like Beethoven's

Ninth when the voices joined in. It just suddenly poured forth; an ode to joy and love and living. The yellow bill would open and close, the small throat tremble, the whole performance completely natural and effortless. No one ever taught a blackbird how to sing.

They always crept home silently after that. A long content; a therapeutic blessing when adolescence brought its turmoil of questioning and riddle. It balanced the seeming insanity of the world and the mean ways of 'people'. What a weary world it could be at times -- at school -- or home.

Unhappiness, though, could never be too long-lasting when they could slope off to hear the blackbird sing. But the contrast often made them ask WHY?

Each spring the blackbirds nested by the tree-house. Each spring as the birds tidied up their old nest the boys would be renovating their hidey-hole as well. The brown hen always seemed to be sitting. Among the shadowy trees, twenty feet above the soft earth, she was often only discernible by the light from her bright, wise eye. The cock bird still sang from his stance each evening. No doubt he also sang at dawn but they were never there to hear him.

In fact, time, once without horizons, was creeping up on them, adding to the disenchantment of the world. Team games demanded such a disproportionate amount of time, and there was always more and more prep. Teachers and parents pushed and pried, planned (and no doubt prayed) over them. All *they* wanted was peace, to be left alone.

The tree-hide was more than ever a sanctuary. In solitary or brotherly contemplation there was peace, usually. Nature never hurried. Life and death and the patient seasons followed in tranquil continuity.

It was about the nadir of their adolescent days when even the world of the blackbirds fell apart.

One day Will noticed a commotion in the nest. The occupants were pretty hefty fledglings at the time and the mother bird was away foraging food for them. Will looked quickly in case an owl or rook was trying to steal a young one. There were no predators about, but the nest was a seething, squeaking, half-feathered riot. There seemed no reason for it, but what caught Will's interest was that one of the blackbirds was white. A white blackbird? It just did not happen!

It was a rather blotchy, dirty white, of course, not commercial T.V. white. Will went rushing off home to fetch Gus.

"A white blackbird? Don't be daft!"

"But it is, Gus!! Come and see."

"I can't."

"Why? It would only take a minute."

"I'm in the middle of prep. Can't you see I've got this bloody algebra to do."

"Och, leave it just now. You can crib mine. I got it off Allan."

"Oh, alright then. But if you're pulling my leg....."

"I'm not. Honest!"

"Mother said we were to stay in."

"She's at the Women's Guild."

It was as Will had described. The whitish chick was smaller than the others and they both decided it was being 'got at' by its brothers and sisters. They seemed to go out of their way to trample it, and when mother or father flew in with food its wide gape always seemed to be missed. The others competed fairly: cheeping and stretching up their opened mouths hopefully -- but at the same time they all seemed to delight in pushing the white misfit aside, or grabbing the very worm from its beak if it was lucky enough to get one. It rather upset the pair, and after an hour, algebra and anything else forgotten, they set off to find Peem.

He was searching the long grass below the second green and watched their approach with mixed feelings. The White boys were a bit skeery these days, he thought -- he never quite knew how to deal with their somersaulting moods.

"Peem, can a blackbird have a white chick?"

-150-

"Aye, but it's very uncommon."

"Well, our one has."

"At the hide?"

"Yep. We've been watching it."

"The others bully it, though."

"They will. It will probably die."

"Die?"

"Because it's different."

"Different?"

"Uh-huh. Nobody likes things that are different. Like me. Whoever invited me into their house? They wink and laugh at me behind their backs or tap their heads...."

"We don't."

"No, maybe not. Maybe you will."

"Never! It's nobody's business. You're just Peem to us and always have been."

".......and always will be."

"You lads make it too easy. The world isn't perfect."

"It should be."

"You see everything in black and white. Later you'll laugh at me because I'm odd -- funny. Like your white blackbird. It sticks out a mile. It's not natural. It would be like an Eskimo coming to live in the village here. It would stick out a mile. Everyone would talk -- peck, peck -- until they drove him away. People don't like what ain't normal, I tell you."

They walked along the bank in silence, kicking at the tussocks. Guys found a ball and gave it to Peem. They stopped at the end of the rough, then sat down above the burn. Voices of kids at play came across from the Mill Green.

"It will die?"

"Uh-huh. Or they'll kill it."

"Who'll kill it?"

"The others. Or the parent birds."

"Just because it's white?"

"Because it's odd."

"Can't we stop it?"

"I don't see how."

They fell silent again.

"Oh well, I suppose we'd better go."

They left Peem, crossed the burn and from the Mill Green cut home through the Old Town.

Mother and father were home and they received a bawling for being out instead of finishing their prep. They went sulkily to bed. They lay watching the play of light on the wallpaper.

"I think we must be odd, too, Gus."

"Why?"

"Nobody seems to be much like us. I'll be glad to get away from here."

"Mm. They do seem to pick on us."

"You'd think we were always wrong or something."

"Well, we're not. It's just a stinking dirty world. It's all wrong. We don't go picking on people. What Peem said was perfectly true. Everyone's got to be goody-goody. Or else!"

"Whoom!"

"Aye!"

"Like we'll get from Speedy in maths tomorrow."

"Oh, to hell with maths."

"Couldn't we feed it extra?"

"We could never reach it."

"Why?"

"The branch would break and it's out of reach any other way."

"They probably chose that site for safety."

"Like everyone else."

"God!"

"Mm?"

"Even birds aren't perfect. Everything in the wood seemed perfect. But birds are just like everyone else. Why does *everything* turn out bad?''

"But there's got to be birds of prey."

"That's different. That's always been."

"How do you mean?"

"Well, what I said. Nobody minds a rook or an owl taking a chick. That's natural. But not blackbird to turn on blackbird. Or man on man."

"But they don't usually."

"They do if they get a chance. Like Peem. Or Lindsay junior. How would you like to be called 'Lip' all the time because you have a funny lip and can't talk properly. Humans are worst of all."

They fell silent. Then one quietly declared:

"I'm not going back to the hide till they've flown. I've lost all faith in anything being decent now."

"Me too."

On which depressing note they fell into the deep relaxed sleep of youth. Missed, too, their parents looking in on their way to bed -- a perplexed, long look of love from the doorway.

"I suppose we should make allowances for them. It can't be easy growing up nowadays."

"Poor dears. They'll soon be wanting to fly their nest."

"They're good boys, darling."

"I know."

The rest of that week was a fair taste of purgatory for the two boys. They were fairly caught by Speedy -- and belted. Gus smashed a table lamp which had been a wedding present and Will caught it for that too, by saying it was 'just an old lamp'.

And on Saturday they both 'excelled themselves', as the games master put it. Will, in an away game, blatantly fouled an opponent and the resulting penalty gave the opposition the game. As the ball soared between the posts, Gus turned on Will sarcastically and Will, sunk in gloom, flew at him. So two minutes from no-side they were both sent off. You simply don't brawl on field in the Second Fifteen.

They returned to the devastating news that Peem had been

knocked down by a van and killed. They had been on their way to find him to pour out the morning's woes. No Peem! They both wept selfishly and sadly, fumed at Colonel Buick at the Golf Club whom they overheard saying he didn't know where he'd get his cheap golf balls in future. They took themselves off to bed early. Clung and cried again like children, cried for the shattered innocence and their own surprising vileness.

"We're as bad as anyone else."

"I wish we'd never been born."

On Sunday morning they blatantly refused to go to church. What did God care?

"But it was only Peem, darling."

They stared, thunder struck.

"Mum!" Will gaped.

"Only!" Gus cried.

They both ran from the house, yelling to shut out their mother's calling them to come back and be sensible.

They scrambled through the ruin and splashed blindly under the bridge. Gus knocked off a thin stalactite and swore viciously. They stumbled out from the dark archway.

The wood lay sunny and cool before them. The burn was low, its laughter muted, the whole place Sabbath-silent. A cushie was quietly coo-ing but the early morning bird activity had stopped. A tree-creeper worked its way up the rough bark of a Scots pine.

The peace of the scene stopped their headlong rush. They stood still. Slowly their panting subsided. Will sighed.

"Mm?"

"It's beautiful, Gus. Just beautiful."

"I know. And it's ours."

They reached the foot of their tree where the old secret hide nestled up among the smooth beech branches. They pulled the ladder out from its hiding place below the elderberries. As they did so a blackbird went clacking off.

"It's only us!" Gus called after it, laughing.

"Look, Gus!"

"What?"

Will pointed.

Ten feet out from their tree lay the soft, crumpled corpse of the white blackbird.

When they looked out from the hide the nest was empty. The birds were away, fledged, vanished into life.

The soft coo-ing of the dove came through the golden morning. They lay strangely soothed and silent until hunger warned it was lunch-time.

"Sorry, Mum. Sorry, Dad," they said as they came in. They looked so grown-up, yet so brittle and lonely.

"That's all right, lads."

"Where were you? Secret Wood?"

"Yes."

After a silence one of the twins said: "The white blackbird is dead too."

"White blackbird? You boys do talk nonsense!"

They glanced at each other.

They did not argue.

Nor did they return to the wood any more.

A BIRD IN THE HAND

Let us call him A.D.; after all, that was what his equals called him, face to face, and what his inferiors called him behind his back. The latter were far more numerous, for A.D. had made his way to the top of 'a well-known company', as the B.B.C. might put it. It was an uncrowded summit.

A.D. was about one and a half stones overweight, had lost most of his hair, wore thick, almost rectangular, glasses and if you think this is a fairly stereotyped description of the boss of a big concern, you are right. A.D.'s was a majesty robed in all the trimmings of real estate. His office could be any one of a thousand others, his secretary one of a few dozen (he had taste in some things), his temper -- ah, now -- there he had a personal and special annoyance, one that would have driven a Trappist to screaming. It certainly caused many changes in the secretarial side and a few nervous breakdowns among the higher echelons in the ante-rooms of power.

He had overcome *their* problem by simply sound-proofing the offending side of the building. But his own office he would not silence. A.D. hated cigarette smoking and always insisted on an open window, even though winter storms might waft snowflakes in upon the most recent company report lying on his desk. He could be very 'thrawn' as he admitted, but, with a disarming smile, put this down to a Glasgow upbringing, a Belfast blossoming and a fight to the top in New York. Anyway, his window stayed open and he suffered the continuous and unique assault on his ears.

Quite often there was a a great deal of noise, anyway. The works were not exactly silent, and though the main floor was on the other side, machinery of one kind or another was usually to be heard and sometimes even felt, as when the big overhead travelling crane went rumbling up high above the main floor, to end just an office away from the boss himself. Often enough he had rushed visitors through to the office window to let them see this great crane at work. It never failed to impress. No, that sort of sound is common enough and soon blends into the background so that only the quivering coffee cup might remind you that giants were at work nearby. The noise that drove strong men crazy was not of man's creation. It was natural.

I do not understand why people go into joyous print at the sound of the first cuckoo. Anyone living in the country groans at its first clear call. If you live next to a wood and possess a shotgun then I reckon murder is justified if the victim is a cuckoo who calls endlessly, not only on the hours but halves and quarters and much else between. Now if cuckoos can drive you mad with their perpetual repetition, pity A.D., who had to put up with worse than those two-stroke pirates. His problem was corncrakes.

Their only resemblance to cuckoos was in their persistence, but to this was added an almost human (ten-year-old's) mechanically-applied menace. Imagine a kid swinging backwards and forwards on an old iron gate which grated and squeaked at each movement. Given an adult nearby, you can be sure that within ten minutes there will be an irate scene. The indulger may not even be aware of his assault, though the victim will be hard to convince. This, rather than the innocent, almost innocuous, cuckoo-call, is the right picture of a corncrake's calling.

When A.D. eventually took his jangling nerves to the ornithological section of his local library he found, resentfully, the following correct, if inadequate descriptions: "Call like the continuous rasping of metal....a ventriloquist effect of constant grating noises....sound like a gate swinging back and forth for hours....difficult to place but a shifting and continuous double rasping sound....recalls a grated comb, its *crex crex* is much more often heard than its brown form is seen......''

He savagely underlined the many repetitions of the word 'continuous'. It was that after all which nearly drove him to resignation. It verged on the edge of the ridiculous. He had been thirty years in the game and now stood among the top ten tycoons in the country -- a perilous post all too often relieved by coronary thrombosis or an overdose of sleeping pills. A nervous breakdown felt more likely in his case.

''Now I know how Moby Dick felt'' he yelled at one hectic board meeting as he slammed the window shut. I hardly think Captain Ahab, or the crew of the *Pequod*, would have felt flattered by being compared to the small, shy, waterbird *crex crex*, but then they have never had to put up with this bird. A wife fractionally as nagging could be divorced on the grounds of cruelty. It was both becoming beyond endurance and beyond understanding. A.D. was being reduced to the ranks by a mere bird.

It showed at that particular board meeting. There was an important takeover bid under way, and, as the firm's first offer had been summarily rejected, A.D. was not in the best of moods. Frequently everyone seemed to be talking at once (and mostly nonsense) or there would be a sullen pause, into which would insinuate the *creak creak* of 'that bloody bird!' It was as if the directors and accountants and secretaries and coffee-makers were all swivelling in squeaky chairs together. *Creak. Creak....*It was a grim meeting.

A.D. insisted they dined out together afterwards, which shows how badly his nerves had been affected. He was normally as canny as a Scottish lawyer. The dinner was to prove more historic than the board meeting. A.D. had swallowed companies before now, and would do so again, but that night saw a file opened on the corncrakes -- literally. It was a buff-coloured one and was not to leave his desk or briefcase for weeks.

John was a friend of mine and as one of A.D.'s staff attended both meeting and dinner. He happened to be an ornithologist. As such he had begun the day delighted at hearing this now rare bird, and amused at the low tolerance-rate A.D. showed towards it, or them rather, for there were usually several 'craking' away at once. By about the fourth coffee stage of the meeting even John had rather gone off corncrakes. Hence his less than tactful words to A.D.later.

"You seem to be rather persecuted by corncrakes, I noticed today. They do go on a bit don't they, sir."

A.D. glared back, so John felt glad he managed a subsidiary company a hundred miles away, but having spoken, he floundered on.

"Have you ever actually seen one?"

A.D. controlled a teetering outburst.

"No, I've never seen one, though I've had a gun by my desk for two years."

At John's look he continued, "I gather you don't altogether approve."

(Answer that honestly, my friend, if you dare!)

Somehow John led the conversation on, to quite unexpected results, for A.D. actually took him in to dinner and placed him at his right hand -- in order to pump him for all he could about this avian brain-washer.

John explained how the corncrake was quite a common bird even a hundred years ago but man, by changing the environment, had steadily reduced their numbers so they were now rare or absent in most districts. They skulked about on wetlands or lush grassy areas, and, being well camouflaged, were difficult to observe. Between 'crakes' they tended to scuttle along -- hence the almost ventriloquist effect. A.D. listened carefully and wrote down the name of one or two bird books. "I want to know my enemy" he joked -- only it did not sound humorous. It amused everyone else though. He might have talked business till all hours, or been moody or in his cups, instead he was obviously interested in what John had to say. The atmosphere grew so friendly that before they separated A.D. had John promising to come up the following Sunday to go on a corncrake-spotting expedition outside the factory.

There were smiles everywhere next day as the account went round. "Can you just see old A.D. squelching about in Wellingtons in the marsh all day?" John's final words to A.D. "You'll need Wellington boots and good binoculars" became almost a catch phrase. They blessed John, for the tenseness had gone out of A.D. and the takeover business. Everyone breathed easier. A.D. spent most of his lunch break actually away from his desk. He stood at the window, peering through big 10 x 50 binoculars, but, as John had warned, saw no sign of the corncrakes.

The next evening he took back several overdue library books and came home with a pile of bird books. The file grew!

"The rasping voice, like a piece of wood continuously drawn over the teeth of a comb, was once common in the British countryside. Only in western parts of Ireland and Scotland does it maintain its hold now." (A.D. added to his notes in red ink 'Springwell is on the east coast. This is personal persecution!')

"Like many of the rails (*Rallidae*) this bird is shy and skulking, its insistent voice announces its territorial claims.

"It feeds in fields of long grass or damp, sedgy meadows and wetter wasteland, feeding on grasshoppers, beetles, earwigs and other insects, slugs, snails, worms and millipedes and some rush seeds.

"*Crex crex* has declined almost to extinction." (A.D. glossed this with a sour 'Hurry up, then!')

When the weekend came John motored up to A.D.'s home. On the Sunday morning they drove off, as one of his children said, 'to go hunting for cornflakes'.

At John's urging they were off early. Not long after they had driven into the works, a patrolman, with an Alsatian dog, accosted them in a remote corner (two tweedy types draped with binoculars and cameras) and despite all protests they were marched back to the security desk at the entrance. A.D. was furious and the poor patrolman much embarrassed when it came out just who he had caught. (To do A.D. justice the next day he sent for the man and both commended and tipped him for his zealous rectitude.)

A.D. had an interesting morning. John was a knowledgeable bird-watcher. It was a hobby he pursued ardently at home and it was also an activity he squeezed into happy moments in many a country while others sat bored over delayed flights and the long waits that go with modern travel. So he was able to show A.D. many things as they patiently stalked the elusive corncrakes. By the end of the morning they had obtained several sightings. A.D. was amazed at the bird's smallness and its unpretentious appearance. Was this really the bird that had been persecuting his office hours?

They repaired to that office for a dram (and for A.D. to empty his Wellington boots). Through the open window the *creak....creak....creak* went on incessantly. As they left A.D. took his gun from a cupboard.

"I don't think I need this any more."

"Do I have a convert to bird-watching?"

"No," A.D. replied, "A gun is no solution, that's all. Might as well shoot at the moon." They drove silently home to A.D.'s house where family lunch rather drove birds from their thoughts. The duck was delicious, the wine a delectable *rosé.* They retired to A.D's study with the coffee tray.

"Now you tell me how to deal with this problem, John," A.D. demanded, but when John left an hour later, A.D. still faced the same problem. He could silence a corncrake no more than Canute could stay the tide.

Time went on. John had almost forgotten about A.D.'s problem, though he should have known better. When the big boss opened a file on anything, or anyone, then it was worked on with remorseless energy.

The phone rang. John stood mentally to attention when a brisk female voice said A.D. was on the line. Without formality their last conversation was resumed.

The voice boomed out triumphantly. "I've got the solution, John, Came to me last night in my bath. Laugh not!" (John wasn't.)

"When I pulled the plug out I suddenly thought 'That's what I'll do to those bloody birds!' Drain the boggy fields next door, man. No marsh, no corncrakes, right?"

John rather glumly echoed "Right." His sympathies lay with the birds.

A.D. soon set the wheels in motion. His secretary found out the land was zoned for industrial use but being so damp nobody was very interested in developing it. It ran down to the sea on the east, the factory occupied its northern edge and south it merged into pleasant agricultural land. A minor road ran on its western edge and beyond that lay miles of pine plantations. There seemed to be no reason why he could not purchase it, though he would have to submit all the usual plans, etc. It would be cheap land at least.

Wryly A.D. told John he would have to think up some idea for its use. There would be a board meeting in a week and he would have it on the Agenda then. "I can hardly put in for planning permission for draining God knows how many acres simply to be rid of some birds. Besides, it's got to pay for itself somehow."

John attended the meeting. It, too, was a rather grim one. A.D. was being pushed to make a third offer on the takeover business. He was in a pugnacious mood. Eventually it was settled, to at last one man's satisfaction.

"Next," A.D. demanded.

With a trace of a smile the secretary announced: "Development of 600 acres, at present marsh and fields, adjoining the Springwell site."

The discussion progressed in what A.D. rudely called 'square circles' and an hour later they had gained no ground whatsoever. They were momentarily silent when John let out a gasp. All eyes turned to him.

"I've just had an idea."

"Out with it then."

John paused, then said, "No, I need time to think first. Could I call in tomorrow and see you, sir, before going south? I may have the perfect solution, but I do need to think first.''

"Well, as we don't seem to be getting one now, tomorrow can only be better. Ten o'clock.''

The rest of the Agenda was rattled through, partly due to A.D. giving it less than his usual attention. He was already imagining the morrow.

When John was shown in at two minutes to ten, A.D. greeted him. "Well, how do I get rid of my bloody birds and still put cash in the coffers?

John almost visibly braced himself, then grinned. "You don't get rid of the birds. You increase them.''

As long as he lives, John will remember the look on the old man's face. For once A.D. was at a loss to say anything. Eventually he croaked, "Increase them? Increase them? Are you going bonkers, or am I?''

"Neither. I reckon we gain back the price of the land in five years and in ten are bringing in a steadily-growing income -- not a fantastic profit, but giving pleasure to thousands, and dealing with your concrake problem''

"Now you're talking in riddles. We make a profit by growing corncrakes?''

"No, not just corncrakes. All kinds of birds. We make it into an ornithological sanctuary, open to the public with hides, exotic foreign species, bookshop, restaurant -- something both lavish and spacious so the birds really have room, yet are shown off to advantage. I've seen it done at Slimbridge in Gloucestershire and in la Dombes in France. Next week, when you are in Lyon, you could go there -- it's only an hour by car --take a look, then comment on my idea. It's not as crazy as you think.''

John had seldom made such a long or such an urgent speech in his life. A.D. remained quite silent. After the long pause he replied. "I don't think it's crazy. It's just way out, man.'' He chuckled. "I like it. I like it. Sure I'll visit that place near Lyon. You be here on the sixteenth, ten o'clock, and meanwhile do me a paper on the sort of things you have in mind.''

"Can I leave that till after you've seen the Dombes, sir. It's what I have in mind, so once you've seen it, we could know where we stand without wasting effort.''

"You know, I like you, lad. You use your imagination and don't mess about.'' He pulled a face. "I don't like writing reports either. Hell, you'd better come with me to Lyon. I can't even pronounce, what's the place Dumbez?''

"Dombes. Parc Ornithologique Departemental de la Dombes to give its full title.''

"If this comes next door you'll have to find a shorter name than that. It's your baby then, John. See my secretary. Fit us in a visit to this bird place. Get on to them. It's all yours until it's proved useless. And, if it's no good, I'll not hold it against you. Bring your wife to Lyon too if you like. It's quite a place.''

A.D. walked John to his car and many employees wondered as he stomped the corridors back to his office -- for he chuckled almost continuously as he walked. Once in his office he took his binoculars out of a drawer and looked out over the marshes. *Crake...crake....* came the call from the invisible birds.

****

Anyone at all interested in birds knows Springwell Sanctuary, either by repute or from a treasured visit. As I live only six miles away I have a 'Friends of Springwell' season ticket, and besides the director is a great friend of mine. He gave up a promising career in industry to develop and run this great sanctuary. John is one of those lucky, happy men who have turned their hobby into a way of life. A.D. I came to know a bit too, as we are both on the Springwell Management Committee. He is Sir A.D. now, of course.

Last week I made my first visit to his office. Having heard so much about it from John I felt I almost knew the place already. The window was wide open. I had to smile (not unnoticed by A.D.) for through the clear east coast air came the faint call of a corncrake.

It was a very *faint* sound now though, because it, perforce, competed with screeching black-headed gulls, honking Himalayan pheasants, screeching peafowl, gabbling ducks and all manner of loud-voiced exotics. but it was still unmistakable: *crake....crake....*

A.D. handed me his binoculars.

THE WINNER

Polly enjoyed her dreams. She only wished the free flow of imagination that occurred in the middle of the night was as regularly enjoyed in daylight hours. Writers' block is, alas, a diurnal disaster.

Sometimes, she could hardly tell whether she was awake or asleep, for the dream would come and go, it would change and develop, with her apparent knowledge that it was happening and apparant control over it, with her directing the twists and turns of the plot. As a writer she certainly relished her dreams, though she sometimes wondered if she was simply carrying her work into the world of sleep. Did mathematicians solve complicated equations at three o'clock in the morning? Was this sort of thing good for you?

Polly kept a pen and pad by her bed in an effort to glean useful copy from this unlaboured field. The annoying thing, of course, was how very difficult it was to retrieve those dreams from the world of sleep. The whole night could go (so it felt) in teasing away at a marvellous dream, one perfect for a short story or sometimes even for the sweep of a novel, but, when she looked at the old maid's scrawl later in the day, there was often little sense in her hieroglyphics or, most annoying of all, the mere reaching for a pen in the dark seemed to wipe the memory clear of the shadowy inspiration. Dreams were damnable the way they kept their Dali-like distance: sharp, clear, weird and inimitable.

Polly seemed to be conscious of all this even as she worried away at one particular dream recently. It was a brilliant dream, all a short story should be, right down to the twist in its tail, which she was sure *she* had dreamt-up (if you see what I mean) rather than dreamed unconsciously. With the carefulness of taking a bone away from a dog, she stole out of the dream then, fully awake, went over it all again. Yes, it was good. She reached for biro and pad and, by feel, scribbled down the key words and phrases, the story's skeleton that would be clothed later in the day. She gave a squawk of glee. *This one had not got away.* She let the pad fall to the floor and smiled off into a smug sleep.

Even the alarm going off was not resented. She danced out of bed, hummed through breakfast, sang through the chores, then went through to her bedroom-study to write 'the winner'. She had not even tried to remember the intricate plot. It was all there, ready to work on. The morning should see it done. She could then justify taking the afternoon off to work in the garden. On some days at least a writer's life was 'a joy bright as summer poppies'.

She picked up the pad. The first few words were clear: "Roofless, dead cottage....." but the rest of the A4 sheet was blank, as blank as her memory of the dream story she had created in the night. After just three words the biro had run out.

DATE-STAMPED

The old man, Dennis Greave, was dying and knew it; his son was alive and didn't know it. Each worried about the other, of course. They had become much closer since Mrs. Greave had run off with someone else and left father and son alone in the big rambling house above Minehead. Daughter/sister Julie had already married and emigrated to New Zealand. She did not know her father was dying. Neither Dave nor Julie would know if he could help it. Come the end of the term Dave set off for the Alps as usual.

He'd gone to visit his father in hospital a couple of days before leaving. Dennis had been propped up on the pillows, reading a hardback Agatha Christie, the regular birthday present from his son. Dennis smiled cheerfully at his offspring, the six foot six genetic hiccup, sprung from parents both a mere five foot six.

Dave slouched in with a deceptive lope. He had to slouch. Ever since he'd shot up over six feet life had given his cranium a variety of blows. "I can't go around wearing my helmet all the time" he'd joked. So he shambled along, as his father called it, but Dennis had learned the hard way that this skinny awkward-looking youth was made of the toughest fibres.

Dave had just gone up to university (Keele) when his mother ran off with a glib car-salesman she'd met in the new supermarket. The young man had been deeply offended, for their upbringing had been very 'middle class virtuous'. He could never decide just what his feelings for his mother had been. She had been a rather distant, hectoring figure, running the household as if it had been a family business. A cold figure, he'd decided. His father, on the other hand, had been -- and was -- warm. The father-children relationship had been much more comfortable. He did not really miss his mother, but worried that she had had that ability to hurt their father. Dennis never talked about the situation. Two years later Julie married and went off to New Zealand, so willy-nilly father and son were thrown together more.

Dave had discovered climbing at university, and all weekends and holidays were spent in Snowdonia or the Lakes or on the spinal Pennine crags that have produced some of England's best gymnastic climbers. Dave was not just a rock climber, though. He liked the mountain atmosphere. ("If it pissed for ever you'd be quite happy ambling along a canal bank" an irate friend once yelled at the end of two days of wet camping at Keswick.) On the other hand he was a good climber, well in the forefront of that surge that followed the breathing space after the Joe Brown years had passed. Because of his restless roaming Dave's routes tended to be all over the place but partners were never difficult to come by; he was naturally gregarious, never seemed to sleep, cooked great grub (after his mother's desertion Dennis told him he'd have to learn to cook in self-defence) and well-enough known for routes on places as far apart as Cornwall and Orkney. He skied in to put up the first winter routes on Creag an Dubh Loch. In his second year he'd discovered the Alps. After that he was never home in the summer.

Dennis did not mind. He had always been deeply involved in his everyday work, proud to be a craftsman rather than just a worker. He had trained as a cabinet-maker (much against the desires of his own ambitious teacher-father) and specialised in ecclesiastical work: everything from rood screens to lecterns and altars to figures of Christ crucified. He'd even decorated the *mirhab* of the new mosque in Bradford and spent a year on restoration work in Dunster Castle. A ducal dining table was much less satisfying however; even if the order would take a decade to deliver; twelve chairs still smacked of the conveyor belt.

Minehead wasn't the most central place to live and work, but the view out from High Town over the channel to the Welsh coast would be sorely missed, and the sheer usefulness of the spacious Victorian monstrosity of a house would be hard to match. And shifting his lumber stocks was out of the question. (He'd accumulated woods from all over the world, every holiday being a buying trip as well as relaxation.)

The children used to draw in great gulps of air every time they left or returned home: enter, and the air bore a pervasive, sweet tang of wood; depart, and one met the freshness of sea breezes. Dave came to think it a pointer that his mother usually wrinkled her nose every time she returned home.

As a boy Dave used to think his father was henpecked, but as he passed through adolescent years he discovered the iron that lay below the veneer of quietude. And Dennis would secretly smile as he saw the same traits emerge in his gangly son. Exmoor gave Dave his love of the open air, so he gravitated to botany and then geology, but, faced with the life-long prospect, however lucrative, of working in the new oil world, he finished his Ph.D. and then started out to be a doctor -- an eye surgeon ultimately -- as this could take him to further distant ranges and would allow him to put something back into those proud but poor places whose peoples he so much admired. The Alps naturally led to further ranges and "he who looks on Nanda Devi will be looking for ever" as he'd heard one of their porters, Sher Singh, remark at Joshimath, during the one Himalayan trip he'd had. (First ascents of Deo Damla and Mangraon.)

Being a perpetual student was very satisfying and his hard work and hard play made for a happy, balanced life wherever he was. Once he'd got his father to come up to the Lakes and a long day over High Street had been the first and last such joint venture. "I don't get you carving a Madonna, lad, and I'm not going to hamstring your mountain strides" Dennis had declared over supper in the Glenridding Hotel.

Mutual respect led to a growing friendship between father and son, a rather rare phenomenon in the fractious sixties. They liked each other's company. They liked the old house. They could talk over pints till all hours or sit before a blaze of scented wood in companionable silence. Dennis also enjoyed meeting the climbing friends or girl friends Dave would bring when climbing on Bosigran.

Dennis had always given Dave his head and if some of the climbing escapades alarmed the old man, he never let on. The idea of Dave eventually serving poor people as a doctor pleased him immensely. He just regretted seeing less of Dave as he was studying medicine at Dundee. "Nearer to the hills" Dave had grinned at his father.

Just after Easter Dennis had gone to the doctor as he had been feeling increasingly poorly for some time. Hearing he'd been 'holidaying' in Turkey the young doctor had done little more than give him a tonic. He did not get any better, in fact he became very much worse, and when, in late June, he was taken to hospital for a real check-up it was to discover bowels and organs riddled with cancer. He said nothing about this in his letters to Dave or Julie, but Dave had naturally called in as soon as term ended. His father did not look too bad and simply wouldn't talk about himself or hear of Dave cancelling his Alps trip. They knew each other too well to argue.

Dave outlined his plans, ambitious as ever, now being into first British ascents or new routes on the Chamonix *aiguilles*. It was an extra agony to smile and smile knowing this was the last he'd see of his son.

He'd made his peace with himself and his work. The big memorial for Wells Cathedral, the finest cathedral in England as he thought of it, would never be completed -- by him. (It was later completed as a a memorial *to him*.) He wrote a long letter to Julie who had gone so far from his life but seemed happily married and 'about time', was going to become a mother. Would he hang on long enough to be a grandfather? He also wrote to his wife but had no address for the letter. He tore it up. How extraordinary, how sad, that such separateness could happen. The mother of Julie and Dave might as well have been dead. Maybe she was. She had vanished, had written one letter, and never been heard of again. Not that he had tried to contact her. He was a proud man.

He still had Dave, however, And even Dave, once well qualified, would wander away. With a pang he realised this was a future he'd never see. Just as he'd never see the old house again. This was his last, very last, contact with all his worlds. This knowledge was his last secret. Best so. We die alone, all of us. Dave was so alive and didn't even know it, racing off to endless living tomorrows while he had mere weeks, or days -- nasty, sordid and painful -- before all the dead tomorrows would swallow him down. Strange how he, the creator of so much of the art of faith, had none himself. Maybe not strange. He had been involved in so many faiths that their colourful lights blazed into one white light in his spectrum of death. It simply did not matter. Dave did, more than anything else in the world.

When Dave's time was up, (''Only ten minutes, Mr. Greave, he has to rest.'') Dave bent over and lightly kissed the bald forehead. The smell of wood was missing, he noted. It was a strange, impulsive act, he thought, as he clattered along the corridor but he didn't see any big deal in it. His father was just so super a person. That he did know.

Dennis watched Dave duck through the doorway and disappear. Proud man or not, he broke then -- for the only time -- and six weeks later was dead. The Agatha Christie was never read.

Dave went out to the Dolomites with two friends and, after a week of poor conditions, had a superb spell of climbing weather. Sated, they moved to Chamonix where conditions were more unsettled but they did get the West Face of the Dru (Harlin, Robbins, Direct), the most sensational new route of the year before. His partners, Pete and Mog, wanted to climb the classic Zmutt Ridge (which Dave had climbed already) so they agreed to meet up again a week later when the others returned from Zermatt.

They had spied a possible new route which Uncle Tom had also outlined in his little note book. ''Och, you buggers are welcome tae it'' he'd grinned. ''Just watch it disna fall doon on top of ye.''

Meanwhile Dave teamed up with Donald Smeaton to have a look at the Requin. They left Snell's Field for the Requin Hut and had only been gone a couple of hours when the weather broke. Tom rather chortled at their discomfort. After several days of rain most people moved on in search of dryer rock. Tom went home. When Dave's partners returned from the -- failed -- Zmutt, two days later, they assumed he was probably stuck on some big route, but couldn't find out where.

They waited a few days but as conditions were good again, left a note and set off for the Italian side of Mt. Blanc. Returning from the Brenva there was still no sign of Dave and there was also a letter for him from his old man waiting at the camp site. Alarm bells were suddenly ringing. Mog eventually telephoned Doctor Tom in Scotland and gained the definite news that Dave and Donald had gone off for the Requin. They had not stayed in the hut but had been seen setting off from the Montenvers.

Several days of searching revealed nothing and it was only a rope of Italians coming down late and their torches failing on the comparatively easy Glacier du Tacul leading them off-route and ending in a silly bivvy that led to the discovery of Dave and Donald. They too must have strayed when the blizzard hit them and in the white-out conditions had fallen into a crevasse -- not the first leading climbers to do so. One of the Italians was airborne, in mid-jump across the crevasse, when he noticed something unusual down in its blue throat.

Dave lay on a ledge, not all that far down, but Donald's body was never recovered. They found a tatty letter written to his father, and a note to Tom, the latter brief enough to quote in full as it explained what had happened.

Your shit route didnt fall on us. We fell in here. On Friday the thirteenth, ha ha. Donald below certainly dead. Dangled for two days with no sign of life so I cut the rope as I couldnt take the st[r]ain any more. Tried cutting holds but dropped the Opinel. No way out. silly way to go. Make it sound easy for my father and sister. They matter more than anything. Feet gone.

Fourth [night] starting. cant hold the [pencil?]

Dave's note to his father eventually reached Julie in New Zealand, along with Dennis's letter to his son. These valedictory letters are too private and poignant to reproduce here, but the superstitious may be interested in one irony. Dennis's letter, from hospital, was written well in advance of his death but with instructions that it was only to be posted when he had died. It bore a clear postmark: BRISTOL, FRIDAY 13th. AUG. 1966.

WESTWARD

Home was the hill and the loch nearby, health was a hound among the stags of the forest, love lay double-folded on the cot, weapons by the doorway, wife by the fire (its flames flickering golden echoes of cornfields among the reek), wind in the heather outby and a wave of the magic dancers over the snowy heights to the north -- HOME was all this world.

But the body lay in pain, no longer a king among beasts, close to the earth-scented undergrowth, not even a child among men. Blood was on his lips and a hot dew damped his brow. How easy it was to lie among the bracken in health, and how impossible for a body of death to find comfort on the softest sheepskins. His wife's hands, strong with seasons, stroked as gentle as the lie of rabbit fur, but to no avail. The fire inside consumed and the fleet man of the hill, the silent hunter of forest and loch, groaned and turned, convulsed like a snared merganser, lost and afraid.

The twins lay in their cot, listening: sleepless, touching limbs for reality, for comfort. They could not understand. Mother moved from fire to bed, the shadows danced, the two cows rustled and aye the wind moved -- like things half dreamed, like longings half lost, the wind came and went.

Moon among the trees, false north light, false stars he cannot see, who like the owl could move as they, silently and sure. Fear lay like the marsh mists of autumn. Fear lay like the deep snow of March. As a hare cringes at the hovering of the hawk there was fear.

When the first golden sunbeam touched the lintel the visitor stooped through the door and entered. The children's eyes grew wide with wonder. The lass sat with the horn spoon between her lips. The boy tried to speak, to bid the stranger welcome, to sit him at the fire, but all he did was stare. The woman it was who bowed before him and said "You have come." He sat and shared the children's meal.

While he supped the mother stood by the bed, rubbing her hands, the hot tears falling on their harsh wringing. She had not spoken again and the children dared not before the stranger in the house. The visitor rose and went to the invalid's rude bed. He touched his forehead gently, whispered soft things unrecognised by the listeners. Their father lay still.

Their mother gasped and made to go to the bed but the stranger held her back, firmly and gently, as a cat can grip a kitten. The invalid opened his eyes and smiled, looked about for a moment, then leaped out eagerly, to embrace his wife who wept with a wild thing's crying.

"The day's work," the man proclaimed, as one who had a harvest ready for the gathering.

"No work," the other replied.

The householder looked at the stranger in surprise, almost as if he had not heard aright, looked too as at the wind; unfocussed, uncertain. The twins wondered indeed if he really perceived him, this man like no other they had seen in their brief springs of life: ageless and strong, with a scent of myrtle and thyme about his garb.

"The hunt then?" The father reached for his bow.

"No hunting."

"Is it war then?" He glanced at the weapons by the wall.

"Not war."

"The fields? The beasts? Woman's work?"

"A journey."

"A journey?"

"Aye, make haste."

The woman was glad to intervene. "You will need food."

"No food, lady!"

Only partly understanding the incomprehensible, he kissed her on the cheek, tousled the children's hair in turn and passed through the door ahead of the stranger, who then strode off, westward along the lochside. He had to stride in turn not be left trailing as a child. In an hour they had passed the loch and the river of the great fish beyond which he had never travelled. Miles of mountain and moor, acres of woods, the lowland bogs and water, all this landscape of diversity fell behind them. As in a dream he saw all his days in the passing but he did not look back.

The two passed through the hills beyond which the sun had set each day, their feet crackled in the red bracken, their breath hung like mist among the rowans, and the snows burned like candles on the altar of the setting sun. They came to the sea where a galley lay beached on the shell sands -- a mysterious, dark shape against the silver seaway to the west.

"Your boat," was the silent indication of the stranger.

"But who shall sail her? My home is the hill. I have no skill in sailing!"

"Oh, you shall sail her. Have no fear. All men sail the boat, at the end, to the westland. Simply bear past the islands yonder then follow the pathway of silver until the sky and sea swamp it out in flames of fire. Follow till the black sail cannot be seen against the starless sky. Farewell!"

The hunter turned his attention to the boat. It was a simple craft but he was no sailor. Pushing off from the shore the currents at once gripped the frail boat and spun it like a winter leaf on the home burn. He tried to hoist the sail and the rope ran through the pulley to collapse the canvas about his head. He fought its enveloping mass in a rising panic.......

.........to find himself grasping the dish-cloth his wife had been banging on his balding head.

"Come on, old man, your coffee's cold! There's dishes to do and the twins to put to bed."

He heaved himself up, placed his book of tales on top of the TV and followed through to the kitchen. This was the worst of a holiday house, even in the romantic west -- a mere change of sinks.

"Remember to go down to Ronnie Mackinnon after. He promised some fresh mackerel tonight."

"Yes, dear."

It was walking along those shell sands with the sun setting beyond the islands, into the end of its path of silver, that he had the queerest notion of fearful familiarity. It was very odd. Ronnie's boat was drawn up, a dark shape, on the sands but the fear kept him from approaching it.

"Come away, Mr. Thompson. I have some fine fish for you tonight," Ronnie called.

He picked his way forward among the rippled ridges and runnels, his heart pounding and his breath short. The man ahead seemed a stranger.

"Are you feeling all right, Mr. Thompson?"

"Deed aye," he grinned, but for the life of him he could not explain just how he did *not* feel all right. It was a shaky hand that reached out for the string of mackerel.

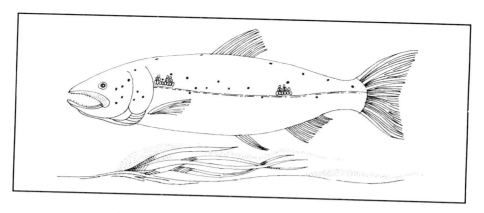

THE FISHERMAN'S RELEASE

The water was clear and cool above the stones, flowing with a quiet laughter, lit by the quivering sunlight that filtered through the trees.

Old Andra leant over the parapet of the footbridge watching the flow, gazing through the crisp movement for the dark grey shapes; but there was only the dappled granite, worn smooth and round, there was only a rusty bicycle wheel to which clung a body of grass and twigs and heather. His eye sought under the peaty bank but no shadow moved there.

He startled at the cry of a hunting kestrel up in the wood and stared into the trees. No bird flew out. Nothing seemed to stir apart from the waters below his feet. The silence and beauty of it suddenly swept over him like a physical thing. He slowly ran his eye over the scene: the long glade, green and bright with soggy sphagnum moss and edged with the purple-brown of heather clumps; dead stumps and fallen trees lay skeleton-white in contrast to the twisted red bark of the old Sots pines and their dark green canopies; the sky beyond stretched lightly blue above the rise of hills. He thought of the Moine Mor up there, the great Moss, the savannahs of space where the turf was soft and the air breezy on the hottest day, where the plaintive cry of the golden plovers wept at the folly of men, and the ptarmigan chicks ran at one's feet. There had been grand days fishing those high hill streams, tasty trout to lay on the scullery slab back in Fife on a Sunday night.

One of the tumbled trees moved though there was no wind -- so he spotted the stag. His weakened eyes could not count its points. It lay quietly, watching the old man, unafraid but cautious, toning in against the heather, its antlers as mossy as the sterile debris of the old forest itself. It belonged to the forest, to the comfort of the trees, it was at home on the long slopes of Beinn Bhreac, in their corries and snow-streaked tops. The old man envied it for the freedom of its ways.

He glanced back to the stream below -- and tensed at once, for a shadow glided out from the rough water where the stream fell to the gorge. It moved effortlessly, slowly bending and unbending its strong shape, nosing up against the invisible current with lithe ease. Andra stood silent, motionless, as the salmon slowly ascended.

He was right above its long grey form, so he could pick out the thrust of its jaw and the impersonal stare of its eyes and the coloured markings along its back.

His sciatica gave a twinge of pain so he jerked back. There was a flash below and the stream ran empty as before. Andra sighed, cursing the weakness of his body. He picked up his rod to move down from the bridge to the great pools of the Linn.

He did not regard himself as really old. Seventy-nine next month. But he had taken it out of himself as a wild youth; he had worked hard, had survived two serious industrial accidents and had been unfortunate in married life. In fact, anyone who knew his wife, Meg Ballantyne, immediately felt sorry for her husband.

The fire had long gone from his soul; the spirit had wilted, the flesh grown weak. His hands, fitting the rod together, shook noticeably.

He had not fished for long when a picnic party arrived, an English family loud with health and jarring laughter. Andra peered unenthusiastically over his spectacles at their advance: cameras and handbags and fancy heels sinking into the peaty soil.

"Daft gowks," he muttered.

They passed without greeting, members of the plastic age, a generation who simply puzzled old Andra. He wished he had got the south bank instead of Archie McLeod -- the road there ran further off among the trees.

"Erchie'll be doon by the Lang Pool," he guessed.

The last member of the picnic party stopped to survey him with the cool curiosity of eleven years.

"Are you fishing?"

"Naw! I'm jist gie-ing me line a wash!"

The boy flushed, stood irresolute for the moment and then fled. Andrew stood cursing himself for an ill-tempered old fool. The hurt was done, however. Too late to call out "I'm sorry, sonny!"

The waters were loud here, bashing their creamy way down worn channels in the grey rock, or lying in golden pools carved out of the granite. One of the greatest salmon rivers in Scotland and he had its freedom, a privilege normally bought for £300 a week; his for the asking in return for a wartime service to the owner.

He remembered when he had been no older than the boy he had hurt. He and two friends had been camping by the Lairig and came on this stretch of falls and pools one evening. They had lain on the smooth, white, sun-warm rocks and watched the monstrous salmon lying in the bottom of the pools. They had bent a safety pin and tied their boot-laces together and 'fished'. They had dangled their lines right before the great creatures, but the fish were wiser than they knew, and it was beans again in the frying pan that night before the long tramp down to Braemore.

"An aw yon laddie kens is sittin on his hunkers in a caur aw day."

He had forgotten his line and the fly lay at the end of the pool dashing from side to side in the rush of living waters.

"It's aw Meg's fault!" he suddenly cried, reeling in.

He had married latish and his choice had been bad. He should have seen the shallow depth behind the young laughter, but he had

-181-

gone headlong and tied himself to the tigress, the tireless nature which had worn down his own. Thirty two years under those claws would have marked the hardiest. Andra had slowly shrivelled and turned grey. At nights he haunted *The Bucking Hind* and at weekends he escaped to the fishing. Anything to be away from Meg. Even that freedom was dearly bought.

"Ye dinna care fir me ony mair. Ye like yir fushin betta," had been his farewell the night before.

It was true, of course. He pictured the return.

"An take yir dirty fish oot of ma kitchen! An look at yir claes! Hoo dae ye think I'll get them cleaned? I'll no be a skivvy fir the likes o you!"

Somehow these days he did not even seem to take many fish home. Not that that made things better.

"Ye gang awa aw weekend and ye dinna even bring a bliddy thing back wi ye. Can ye no even catch a supper noo?"

Perhaps Archie would give him one of his basket. He was a wily lad who always had a good catch, for all he was just forty and new to the game.

Archie had come to live next door and had a car in which he gladly took old Andra in return for being taught the grand game. Pupil, though, had long passed master.

Andra remembered his line again. His cast was a bad one, striking the polished rock on the far side. He tried again and felt the old thrill as it landed fair and floated down through the bubbles into the deep pool.

"Aw, it's graun just tae be here."

Archie and he had come up to the wee hamlet at ten the night before; to Mary Macdonald's, with Mary herself soon producing tea and scones, with the same bedroom under the slope of the roof, the same remembered view over fields to the river and the wide heather hills. It was the pattern of escape built over recent years. Mary understood. It was easy to stand in the kitchen door after supper while she bustled about -- and unburden the cares of life. The menace of Meg seemed remote in that warm place.

Andra always lay in bed there with a great content -- savouring the unusual peace, the absence of a nightly nagging, the blessed noises of the highland dusk: the call of the black-headed gulls or peewits or oyster-catcher, and in the autumn, the distant challenge of the stags, and at all times, the muted flow of the great river, freed from its mountain swiftness and the wanderings in the big forest. He would watch the lace curtains billow and rattle on their rail, gossamer-like in the moonlight. The wrinkles would ease their grip from his face and the dreams were always of long ago.

The Leven had been his earliest playground, and then he discovered the Ochils on the edge of Fife and their hill burns. When he had served his time a gang of them from the mill had bought the rights to Lochan Uaine in Glen Bhuidheanaich. Halcyon days, only given up for the pretty face of Margaret Lamont, willingly given, for Andra held little back.

His rods went into the loft and his waders were more often used on the potato patch between the house and the track out to the pit bing. But how quickly it had spoilt; Meg's impatience and temper, endless quarrels. And childless.

Andra reeled in again and changed flies. A Butcher would be better for the Long Pool. He would fish opposite Archie for a while, enjoying his portly, friendly presence, yet separated by the width of water and the roar of the Linn. He picked his way carefully along the path until he reached the Long Pool. Archie was there sure enough and they waved to each other and Archie shouted something that the older man could not catch, but he smiled in return. Archie held up two fingers.

"Ach, he's fir the Fife Cup this year," sighed Andrew -- without envy. (A. Ballantyne, be it said, was engraved on the cup opposite the dates 1920, 1923, 1924, 1937 and 1946!)

He enjoyed the Long Pool with its shady trees. He felt the peace of the forest again seeping into him. He had meant to see if the stag had moved when he left the footbridge, but had forgotten. It was so easy to forget these days.

"Aye, an ah shid jist forget tae gang hame as weel," he said aloud, and then felt aghast at the very idea, at its impudent possibility.

Why not?

"Jist think, Andra lad: nae mair from the auld girner." Then with a frightened glance round he added, "Gawd, if she kent whit ahm thinkin the noo!"

He cast violently, splashily, so Archie noticed, but the train of thought had entered the long tunnel of his stolid reasoning. Why did he put up with it? With her? But to do otherwise was the notion that shocked him.

"I've aye done the dacent thing."

He watched the pool, pondering. Its quicksilver light flickered back off his wizened face. He looked round at the deep forest. He squinted up into the blue cloudless sky. Here was content.

"Sax bob a nicht at Mary's...that's...twa pun a week maybe. I could dae it tae."

He pulled out a handkerchief and dabbed at his brow. The hand was very shaky.

"Gawd, man, tak a grip of yirsel!"

But the idea would not go. It broke out with a roar in his ears and its sudden sunshine of madness struck like a blow.

HE WOULD NOT GO HOME!

After supper Andra and Archie always went 'fir a wee daunder'. Archie normally had to contain himself for Andra's slow steps but this night he was soon crying:

"Hey, Andra, haud yir horses, mun!"

Normally Andra was full of talk but this night he was silent and withdrawn, yet with his face alight as Archie had never known it.

Mary would have said he was 'fey'; Archie being a right Fifer was merely puzzled and, as he later admitted, "a wee bitty worried."

"Whit's gat intae ye the day? Ye fished the Lang Pool like I've never seen onybody fish. (Five salmon, the heaviest 14 pounds, as against Archie's early two.) Ye scoffed aw the currenty-loaf at tea and ye're walkin me aff ma feet."

Andra laughed.

"Tell ye the morn. I've got a graun notion."

Inside he was simply stomping along, singing "I'll no gang hame! I'll no gang hame!...."

How could he tell Archie?

He would have to tomorrow, for they always left after an early high tea in the front room Mary used on Sundays. His thoughts ran on --

"Erchie will dae his nut! an Meg!...." He laughed outright.

Archie frowned at the old man. He had never known him like this.

"Aye, old Meg! Well, she can just hae some o her ain medicine!"

He smiled at the marshalled trees behind the wobbly deer fence. He could have danced had he known how. Instead he strode along with his head thrown back and arms swinging. He had not felt so energetic or free since he came to the hills as a boy.

"I can bide jist as ah like and dae aw the things she's aye stapped. I'm free!"

And he really believed it.

They walked down to the old chief's castle and back. Mary commented on Andra's flushed appearance.

"You have been doing too much this day, Andrew Ballantyne."

"Ach, awa! I've never felt betta!"

"Whae caught aw the fush, may I ask?" he poked at Archie.

Archie smiled wanly. "He's got a secret, Mary, he'll no let on aboot. I dinnae ken, he's near walked me intae the grun. An he's been laughin awa tae hisself aw day.''

"Weel, sup yir milk and off to bed with the both of you.''

They complied happily enough, like tired youngsters on a summer holiday evening, lost in their own thoughts, dreamily, untidily scattering their clothing and snuggling down in the cool linen.

Moonlight and the gentle flow of waters. Lace curtains swaying in the ghost of a breeze. Waking slid into sleeping before the first owl's call and dreams soon set smiles on their faces.

Archie woke once in the night to hear old Andra talking in his sleep:

"I'll no gang hame! I'LL NO GANG HAME!''

Archie thought, "I widna blame ye; wi yon auld witch waitin,'' and was soon thoughtlessly asleep again.

He woke later than usual. Andra normally woke him. He felt a bit annoyed.

"Hey, Andra! It's time we were up,'' he called across the room. But Andra did not answer -- nor ever would -- and his cry in the night had been very truth.

HE'D NO GANG HAME!

****

It was neighbourly Archie who arranged the funeral, and it was friend Archie who inserted the column in the local paper:

"Andrew Ballantyne, the well-known angler from Calton, died peacefully in his sleep last Sunday morning, while staying at Inverspee in the Cairngorms. He was 78. As a young man he had an international reputation and was President of the Fife Association from 1938 to 1946, when he characteristically ended his extended presidency by winning the Fife trophy for the fifth time. His many friends, young and old, will miss his cheery company, and to his wife, Margaret, we extend our sympathy in her bereavement.''